MURDER AND THE MONKEY BAND

A High Desert Cozy Mystery - Book 1

BY

DIANNE HARMAN

Copyr/ight © 2015 Dianne Harman

Published by: Dianne Harman
www.dianneharman.com

Interior, cover design and website by
Vivek Rajan

ISBN: 978-1517381004

CONTENTS

Acknowledgments

1   Chapter One   1

2   Chapter Two   7

3   Chapter Three   11

4   Chapter Four   16

5   Chapter Five   20

6   Chapter Six   23

7   Chapter Seven   29

8   Chapter Eight   34

9   Chapter Nine   38

10   Chapter Ten   42

11   Chapter Eleven   46

12   Chapter Twelve   51

13   Chapter Thirteen   55

14   Chapter Fourteen   59

15   Chapter Fifteen   65

16   Chapter Sixteen   68

17   Chapter Seventeen   72

18   Chapter Eighteen   75

19   Chapter Nineteen   81

20 Chapter Twenty   86

21 Chapter Twenty-One   92

22 Chapter Twenty-Two   98

23 Chapter Twenty-Three   103

24 Chapter Twenty-Four   107

25 Chapter Twenty-Five   112

26 Chapter Twenty-Six   117

27 Chapter Twenty-Seven   125

28 Recipes   129

29 About Dianne   135

ACKNOWLEDGMENTS

As I write this I think what an adventure this last year has been and none of it would have happened without you, my loyal readers. I was drinking coffee in bed at a resort in Arizona when I jotted down a few ideas for a cozy mystery that had come to me in the middle of the night. When I returned home, I decided to write a book in that genre. That was the birth of Kelly's Koffee Shop. People kept telling me they wanted to read more about Mike and Kelly, so I began writing more books and called it the Cedar Bay Cozy Mystery Series.

I was curious what would happen if I started a different series, and so I wrote Murder in Cottage #6, the first of the Liz Lucas Cozy Mystery Series. Several years ago I worked as an antique appraiser, and I decided to write a book with an antique appraiser as an amateur sleuth set in the community of High Desert, outside of Palm Springs. This book is the first in my new High Desert Cozy Mystery Series.

I've never had so much fun, and there are a few people I need to thank for making it possible. First of all you, my readers, for following me, reading my books, and even contacting me with suggestions. Secondly, my husband Tom, who makes it easy for me to write by taking care of all the things that need to be done around the house. And of course, my cover artist and formatter, Vivek Rajan. It's interesting that I've never met him or talked to him, yet I consider him to be a friend. This is an Internet relationship, and I rather doubt we will ever meet, but I credit him for creating the fabulous book covers that make my work look good.

My family has been so supportive. I love it when I pick up my six year old granddaughter from school to take her to tap dance class and she regales me with a new Puppy Story (the name of the book she wants me to write). They always start out the same way: *It was a long, long time ago in 1956*. I have yet to figure out why she's chosen 1956!

Again, thank you all for making this time of my life so wonderful!

Newsletter
If you would like to be notified of my latest releases please go to www.dianneharman.com and sign up for my newsletter.

DIANNE HARMAN

CHAPTER ONE

Marty Morgan stood in the courtyard of the walled-in housing compound and marveled once again at how lucky her sister had been to find this enchanting place to live in the remote California desert town of High Desert. The peace and tranquility of the desert was a soothing elixir for Marty considering what she'd been through during the past year. Becoming a permanent resident of the laid back community of High Desert, population 7,000, was just what she needed. It provided lots of time for her to relax and concentrate on restarting her career as an art and antique appraiser. While the town was small and only the most essential goods and services were available, the well-known cosmopolitan California desert golfing mecca of Palm Springs was only twenty miles away.

It had been an interesting year for Marty. When her sister Laura had called telling Marty she had a premonition that Marty and Scott were getting divorced, she was reminded once again that Laura had what some called a psychic gift. Even when they were kids Laura would tell Marty about things that were going to happen in the future, like the time she'd foreseen great-aunt Ruth's death. It happened so often Marty took it for granted. It was only after they'd been apart for many years that she realized the enormity of Laura's powerful psychic abilities.

Marty remembered when Laura had been a student at UCLA, and she was asked to take part in a paranormal study conducted by the psychology department. She'd been subjected to numerous tests, and when the testing was finished the psychology department determined Laura had a very high level of psychic abilities which simply couldn't be explained. They told her she possessed what was commonly called a "sixth sense."

During the telephone call with Laura, Marty confirmed what Laura already knew, that she and Scott were getting divorced. Laura insisted Marty move from her home in the Midwest to the little town of High Desert where Laura made her home. Laura told her one of the houses in the compound she owned was going to be available in two weeks, and she was sure she could get Marty some antique appraisal referrals through the insurance company where she worked. Marty didn't need to think twice about the offer. She knew she could no longer live in the small Midwest town that had been her home for the past twenty-five years.

Marty was shocked and dismayed when Scott confessed to her he was having an affair with his secretary, and he wanted a divorce, so he could marry her. He'd given Marty a large monetary settlement and agreed to pay her monthly alimony. She knew it was guilt money, but she felt she deserved it for probably having been the laughingstock of the little town where they lived. Now she understood why so many conversations had come to an abrupt halt when she walked into a local shop. She knew they were talking about the affair and the pending divorce. The little town didn't have many scandals, and Scott's affair with his secretary had provided the residents with a lot of fodder. Marty was certain she was the only one in the town who hadn't known about his infidelity.

She'd lived in the High Desert compound now for almost nine months. One of the residents, John Anderson, owned a fire engine red food truck called The Red Pony which he drove daily into Palm Springs. It had become a popular destination for office workers in downtown Palm Springs to go for lunch. John was an excellent chef, and the entrees he sold from the truck were delicious. When he returned to the compound each day in the late afternoon, the truck was almost always sold out of food. He eagerly sought out people who were willing to try his new dishes before he put them on The

Red Pony menu, and Marty was always the first one to raise her hand when he asked for volunteers.

Max Samuels was John's assistant cook and kitchen helper. Although he didn't live in the compound, he joined the residents for dinner at the compound almost every night. John liked to have him there to help with the new dishes he planned to put on the food truck's menu. When Max helped prepare the new dishes, it really cut down on the instructions John had to give him when they were filling customer's orders. Max was what a lot of people would call a "redneck." He'd lived in the small desert town all his life. There wasn't much work available in town, and Max would never have made it working in the big city of Palm Springs. His country language and lack of social graces would have been major stumbling blocks for him in a city known for its sophisticated and wealthy residents. Being the assistant cook in a food truck was the perfect occupation for him.

Les Richardson was the fourth compound resident. He was Laura's long-time boyfriend and an artist well-known to the gallery owners in Palm Springs. He far preferred the small town residents of High Desert to the "beautiful people" who came to Palm Springs to play golf and brag about their condominiums in the desert when they returned home, although he certainly wasn't averse to them taking one of his paintings with them.

As Marty looked around the compound, her senses fully appreciated what someone had the foresight to build many years earlier. Four small two bedroom houses, built very close to each other, formed a square around a central courtyard. The compound was surrounded on all sides by a rock wall constructed from local volcanic rock.

A large tree that was located in the middle of the courtyard was covered with hundreds of twinkling lights. At night it provided a magical setting along with the lanterns which Laura lit every evening at dusk. Marty had grown to love the muted lights of Palm Springs in the distance and the mauve desert sunsets. A picnic table was situated in the compound, and most of the evening meals were eaten there. Another table was used by the four residents for newspapers, mail, and the food that John cooked, so he could serve it buffet style when he chose to. Even though each of the housing units consisted of separate free-standing house, there was a communal feel to the compound, and the four residents who lived there had grown to truly care for one another.

John's home had been upgraded with a state-of-the-art kitchen, and Les had a large airy, light-filled room which he used as his art studio. When Marty had taken up residence in the compound, about the only things she'd brought with her besides her personal effects were reference books dealing with art and antiques. She'd made the second bedroom in her home into a library/office. She didn't want any reminders of Scott, so she let him keep all the furniture and furnishings they'd accrued during their twenty-five year marriage.

With a smile on her face, Marty looked at the big black Lab she'd bought when she'd arrived in High Desert. She'd needed something that was just hers and Duke, the little Labrador puppy she'd fallen in love with at the animal shelter, had been perfect for her. They'd bonded from the first moment she'd looked into his big brown eyes. Everyone in the compound knew if they saw Duke, Marty had to be nearby. He never left her side, and when she was gone, his eyes never left the road he knew she would use when she returned. The other three residents of the compound were equally enchanted with the friendly lab, and all of them kept a bowl of dog treats handy for him when Marty was gone.

Marty couldn't remember a time she hadn't been interested in art. Her first grade teacher had been amazed at Marty's art ability and had told her parents she loved art so much she could probably benefit from art lessons. Her mother had found an artist who was willing to work with the young girl, and for many years her parents had taken her twice a week for art lessons with the well-known artist. In high school it was always Marty who was in charge of anything art related, from the backdrops for school plays to the posters for the car washes.

Her friends and family assumed Marty would become an artist. She majored in art in college and then abruptly in her sophomore year she changed her major to art history. Everyone was shocked and asked her why. She always replied, "I just didn't have the fire in my belly to make it as an artist, simple as that." She went on to get a master's degree in art history and took a job with an antique and fine art auction house in Los Angeles. When she and Scott got married and moved to the small Midwestern town, she decided to open an art and antique appraisal service and over a period of time developed a thriving business in that area of the state.

The insurance company Laura worked for, Alliance Property and Casualty Company, specialized in insuring personal property items such as art, antiques, jewelry, and other types of high value personal property items. True to her word, Laura's insurance company had been able to refer business to her. Laura worked for a man named Dick Cosner, and one of his jobs was to determine which of their insureds needed to have their personal property items appraised. Many of Alliance's insureds were very wealthy and had brought some of that wealth to the desert with them. They wanted their home in the desert to reflect their wealth and economic status, and many of the homes were filled with antiques and fine art. That was the main reason there were so many art and antique shops in Palm Springs. Dick had referred a lot of business to Marty since she'd come to the area, and she knew she was very fortunate to be able to have an in with an insurance company who needed her services.

Dick Cosner had called Marty earlier in the day and asked her to meet the following morning with the son of a woman who had been murdered the week before. The woman's son, Jim Warren, had called Dick and told him he needed to have the contents of his mother's house appraised for probate. He said he didn't think her Will would be contested, but in case it was, he thought it would be wise to have everything appraised. He knew his mother had gotten an insurance appraisal several years earlier, and he wanted to get in touch with the person who had originally appraised the items. Dick told him that person had left the area, but he highly recommended an appraiser by the name of Marty Morgan, and that she'd been appraising for many years and was very knowledgeable about the values that needed to be established for estate purposes.

"Marty," Dick had said when he called earlier that day, "I'd like you to meet with Jim Warren at this address tomorrow. His mother, Pam Jensen, died recently, actually she was murdered, and she was one of our insureds. I don't know the specifics, but I seem to remember his mother mentioning there was bad blood between her children and her husband's daughter. It was a second marriage for both of them, and evidently there was no amicable blending of the two families. Her husband, Brian Jensen, owned a well-known restaurant in Palm Springs that became so successful he opened a number of them throughout the world. I'm sure you've heard of them. It's the Mai Tai Mama's chain. Anyway, he died a few months ago. Brian was quite wealthy, and he and his wife had been married for almost twenty-five years. I took a look at the appraisal that was done a few years ago, and in addition to numerous antiques and fine art, she had one of the finest collections of 18th century Meissen china in the world. It should be an interesting appraisal. Let me know what you find out."

"Will do, Dick, and thank you so much for the referral. Sounds like something I'd enjoy. I've appraised a number of Meissen pieces and to have a chance to appraise a top collection is a once-in-a-lifetime thing for an appraiser. By the way, would it be okay with you if Laura goes with me? To be honest, I've never done an appraisal when someone has been murdered, and I'm a little spooked by it. This is a first for me."

"Sure, take your sister with you. I'll give her some paid time off from her work here at Alliance while she's helping you with the appraisal. You'll do fine, but keep in mind the fact that the owner of the property you're going to appraise was murdered isn't relevant to the fair market value of the items. Remember that," he said.

"Thanks. I will."

CHAPTER TWO

Jim Warren's adult years had not been kind to him. It seemed no matter what kind of business or relationship he got into, the businesses failed, and the relationships sputtered and died, including two marriages, both of which ended in divorce. The only good thing that happened to him during those years was when his mother married Brian Jensen, the co-owner of the wildly popular world-wide restaurant chain known as Mai Tai Mama's which he'd started in Palm Springs. His biological father had been an alcoholic who had walked out on the family, leaving his mother to work in the shoe department in a high-end retail store to put a roof over their heads and food on the table. That's where she'd met Brian Jensen.

He was nice enough to me. He even gave me money to fund a couple of my companies, but when the last one went belly up, he told me he'd never again give me so much as a penny, and he made mom promise she wouldn't help me financially either. From time to time when mom saw how much I was struggling she'd give me some money, but she always made me promise I'd never tell Brian, and I never did.

Brian had passed away a few months earlier. Jim thought back to a recent conversation he'd had with his mother about Brian. She told him Brian had willed his entire estate to her and deliberately left his daughter, Amy, nothing. Pam told him she felt guilty about that and was going to revise her Will to include Amy. In her new Will, Jim and his sister, Marilyn, who was married to a wealthy private bank manager with J.P. Morgan, would get half of her estate, and Brian's daughter, Amy, would get the other half. Pam said she felt sorry for Amy and even though she'd sided with her mother when Brian divorced her to marry Pam, she shouldn't be punished. Pam said she didn't feel right giving it all to her children, when Brian was the one who had made the money. She'd reminded Jim that she'd brought almost nothing into the marriage.

A bitter argument had ensued with Jim pointing out to his mother in the strongest words possible that if she changed her Will she would not be doing what Brian, her deceased husband, wanted. She countered by saying that sometimes it was more important to be fair than to blindly do what someone wanted done. When the argument ended, Jim left her home in a rage.

It's bad enough that under her existing Will I'm going to have to split her estate with Marilyn, and I'm only going to get half of the estate. If she makes a new Will and Amy gets half, that reduces my share to one-fourth, and that's simply unacceptable. I've got some great plans for a new business here in Palm Springs, but it's going to take a lot of money, money that will now go to Amy if mom carries through with her plan and makes a new Will. I've got to do something to stop her from carrying out this foolish idea she has about trying to be fair to Amy.

Early the next morning Jim called his mother and said, "Hi, mom, sorry about our argument yesterday. I want to apologize for acting so badly. It was just such a shock to think you'd do something that Brian clearly did not want done. Have you thought any more about it?"

"Yes, and although I'm sorry you feel the way you do, I think Brian made a mistake when he left Amy out of his Will. I clearly was the other woman, and I have no idea how much psychological damage the breakup of the marriage did to Amy, but I'm sure there was some. I know this isn't going to make you happy, but I have an appointment with my attorney later this week, and I'm going to change my Will. Brian was a wealthy man, and there will still be plenty for everyone."

"Well, it's your money and your decision. If you feel it's important to do that, I'll respect your wishes. Are you still planning on me being the Executor?"

"Yes, you live locally here in Palm Springs. Since Amy's in San Francisco and Marilyn's in Los Angeles it would make sense for you to take care of it."

"As healthy as you are, I'm sure that won't be something I'll have to do for a long, long time. Love you! Gotta go."

He ended the call. *Sorry I have to do this, Mom, but I'm only doing what Brian wanted.* Jim walked over to his desk, unlocked the center drawer and withdrew the Will his mother had given him for safekeeping several years earlier. He read it to make sure the Will stated that he and his sister, Marilyn, were named as the only beneficiaries other than his mother's long-time housekeeper, Rosa, who was to be given the sum of $25,000. He considered forging his mother's signature on a new Will that left Marilyn out, but he couldn't think of a way to do it that wouldn't cause his sister and brother-in-law to make life very difficult for him and which might ultimately cause him to be exposed as a forger.

There's nothing else I can do. If she draws up a new Will, I'm down to one-fourth of her estate. If I'm going to do something about it, it's got to be done in the next couple of days, before she goes to see her attorney.

Jim walked over to one of the walls in his home office and removed the painting that hung there. He twirled a combination lock on the wall safe hidden behind the painting and opened it. For a moment he stood there and simply looked at the .9mm pistol in the safe.

Fortunately I know the code to turn off the alarm system in her home, and even though Mom's been talking on and off about getting a dog, right now she's by herself, and that will make this ugly little task pretty easy. I should be able to get in and out with no problem. I never thought I'd have to use this pistol on my mother, but then again, I've been planning on this money for a long time, and I'm not willing to give half of it away to Amy. She'd probably go through it all in a few months, giving it away to one of those non-profit organizations she's so involved with.

CHAPTER THREE

Henry Siegelman looked out the window of his La Quinta home, a wealthy enclave on the outskirts of Palm Springs, California, and thought about what he needed to say to Pam Jensen when he called her. Satisfied, he dialed her number.

"Hello, Pam, it's Henry Siegelman calling. I was wondering if you've given any more thought to what we talked about last week."

"I'm not ready to sell, Henry, and I doubt that I ever will be," she said. "We've had this conversation more times than I care to remember. I love my Meissen china collection, and I have no intention of selling it. I'm sorry, but it's a hobby and an investment that brings me a great deal of pleasure."

"Look, Pam, we both know we probably have the two best private Meissen collections in the world. My collection is my life. If you won't sell me your entire collection, at least sell me the three pieces you have of the Monkey Band that I need to finish my set. You'll be a wealthy woman if you sell them to me."

"I'm already a wealthy woman, Henry. This is the last time I want to hear from you. I'm willing my collection, including the pieces from the Monkey Band to my children, and they can decide what to do with it when I die, but according to my doctor, that shouldn't be for quite awhile. I appreciate your persistence, but this subject is finished.

Good-bye."

After the call ended Henry walked over to the wall where he'd installed custom-made glass-fronted shelving. His Meissen china collection was dramatically displayed on shelves which stretched thirty feet along the wall and were five rows high in the family room of his spacious home. Special lighting had been installed that cast a soft light on the various pieces of his collection, highlighting the magnificent colors and designs. The shelving had been bolted to the walls to make it earthquake proof, and he had carefully secured each piece to the shelving with a special wax made specifically to keep displayed antiques and collectibles in place.

Henry had become interested in Meissen china when he was an art history major in college many years ago, and a professor had shown the class a slide show of different types of china and their history. He'd been away at college when both of his parents had died in a tragic home fire, and as the only child of the union, he'd inherited a great deal of money.

Shortly after graduating from college he'd gone to the Meissen museum in Germany and spent days studying all the various types of Meissen china and the different marks on the backs and bottoms of the pieces that indicated a fake from an authentic piece of the hard paste porcelain. The Meissen signature logo was crossed swords in a blue underglaze, and once you'd seen the original mark, it was fairly easy to spot a fake. Although China had started producing hard-paste porcelain in the 8th century, it wasn't until 1708 that the first European hard-paste porcelain was produced at a factory in Meissen, Germany.

The European aristocracy quickly embraced the detailed landscapes, port scenes, animals, flowers, and courtly scenes depicted on most of the Meissen pieces. There was a strong Asian influence in much of the work, as there was in many of the decorative items of the time. The broad palette of colors was appropriate for the bright colors which dominated the 18th century costumes and decorative arts. Small figurines and animals were very much in evidence during this time as well as all types of dinnerware.

Soon Henry felt confident enough to begin buying, and within a few years he'd amassed a large collection of early Meissen pieces. He began employing people in different countries around the world who went to auctions and galleries and bought Meissen pieces for him after he'd researched the sale prices. His reputation for owning one of the finest Meissen collections was well known in the world of antiques.

Henry had been approached many years earlier by a man who had offered to sell him a very important 18th century Meissen piece. Henry researched it and found out that it was stolen. He'd bought it anyway, and it was soon followed by other stolen pieces he'd added to his collection. After all, he reasoned, his collection was just for him, and he was the only person who gained satisfaction from looking at the uniquely beautiful pieces. He had no need to share it with others, and over the last few years most of his purchases had come from the black market rather than being purchased from galleries or at auctions. It was enough for him to know that he was the one who possessed the pieces.

He remembered when an intermediary had first contacted him and offered him several pieces of the Meissen Monkey Band. The pieces had been made in the original 18th century molds in 1746 and were almost impossible to purchase on the open market. The Monkey Band was created by Johann Joachim Kaendler, the most celebrated and famous of the Meissen sculptors. The Monkey Band consisted of a twenty-two piece set of figurines, each approximately five inches in height, depicting monkeys dressed in colorful costumes playing various different musical instruments. They were based on the satirical illustrations of the French artist Christophe Huet and included the monkey conductor of the band who was whimsically perched on the shoulders of another monkey as he directed the band.

Each piece was created in the "singerie" style of elegant monkeys which was very popular with the French aristocracy during the 18th century. He couldn't explain why, but he became absolutely infatuated with the Monkey Band figurines from the moment he first saw them. Privately he wondered if he'd lived in that century and had something to do with the Monkey Band. He'd even wondered if he'd been Kaendler and now was reincarnated as a wealthy man, so he could buy his previous work. That was something he kept to himself, rather certain that people wouldn't understand that type of thinking.

Original pieces dating from mid-eighteenth century in perfect condition brought about $75,000 to $80,000 for each of the twenty-two pieces of the Monkey Band and that was when they were available, which was rarely. There had been a theft of some eighteenth century Monkey Band pieces, and the theft had been written up in numerous antique magazines. The owner had posted a large reward for their return. Henry had been very pleased that he was the one the intermediary had contacted about the stolen pieces. Those were the first pieces he'd bought of the twenty-two piece Meissen Monkey Band. After he purchased the first Monkey Band pieces, he'd become consumed with wanting to own the entire Monkey Band set and within a few years he'd been able to collect all of them with the exception of three pieces: the hurdy gurdy player; the conductor of the band; and the bagpiper. His Meissen collection was his passion, or as the French would say, his *raison d'être*, meaning his reason to be. Ever since he'd learned that Pam Jensen had the three pieces which would complete his Monkey Band collection, he had spent almost every waking moment of the day thinking about how he could get them. He was desperate to own all twenty-two pieces of the Monkey Band.

She's made it very clear she's never going to sell them to me, but I hear her son Jim is money hungry. If something happened to her, I might be able to buy the pieces from him, Henry thought.

He sat for a moment thinking about the steps he needed to take to complete his collection, and then he picked up his phone. "Nick, I have a job for you. It involves a little more than what you've done for me in the past, but I'll make it worth your time." He listened for a moment and said, "Come to my house this evening, and I'll give you the particulars."

Henry smiled thinking about what it was going to feel like when he finally owned the complete set of the 18th century Meissen Monkey Band. He looked at the other pieces of his Monkey Band collection and visualized how the missing three pieces would look in his glass-fronted display case.

It's too bad, but Pam will simply be collateral damage, and that happens in the world of high stakes antiques. She should have taken me up on my offer. At least she would have lived if she had.

Henry had briefly considered having Nick steal the pieces he wanted, but he knew that sooner or later he might be questioned because everyone in the antique world knew that Henry Siegelman wanted those pieces to complete his Meissen Monkey Band. If Pam was murdered and the entire Monkey Band was stolen, no one would point a finger at him.

CHAPTER FOUR

"Rosa," Pam Jensen said as she got ready to go shopping, "I know I tell you this every time I see you dusting my Meissen Monkey Band pieces, but it always makes me nervous. You know how much I trust you, but those pieces are so special to me, and evidently to a few other people as well. Please be extra careful with them when you're dusting. As I've probably told you before, Brian surprised me with them many years ago. I'd mentioned to him how charming I thought they were, and that I'd love to add them to my collection of other Meissen pieces. Without telling me what he was doing, he found someone in China who had a set and bought it for me as a surprise gift on our tenth anniversary."

"I know how much you love them, Mrs. Jensen, so I'm special careful with them. Don't you worry."

When Pam was gone Rosa took a long look at the Monkey Band pieces. She agreed with what Mrs. Jensen had said – the pieces were special. In fact so special that yesterday a man had offered Rosa a great deal of money if she would turn off the security alarm when she left for the evening, so he could get into the house and steal the pieces. He'd paid her $5,000 as hush money and told her there would be another $45,000 for her if she agreed to do it. She liked Mrs. Jensen and didn't want to jeopardize her job, but with Julio out of work, money for their family had really gotten tight. Even though Mrs. Jensen paid her well, it wasn't enough to support the two granddaughters she and Julio were raising plus themselves. She felt her blood pressure rise just thinking about her daughter abandoning her two little girls to go off with that good-for-nothing drug addict.

Like he would be any different from the rest of the men she'd had relationships with over the years. I don't think she even knows who the father is of those little girls. No one is ever going to give me the Mother of the Year award for raising her. Maybe that's why God gave me those two little granddaughters. Sure hope I do a better job with them than I did with their mother.

Maybe I should take the money. Mrs. Jensen would never know about it, and we sure do need it. I told him I'd call him today and give him my answer. I feel guilty even thinking about it, because I know how much Mrs. Jensen loves those Monkey Band pieces, but she has so many other Meissen pieces I don't think it would really matter if a few of them are gone.

When I told Julio last night about the man who offered me the money, he told me he thought I should do it. He said he didn't know how much longer we could hang on. I don't know what to do. I've always been so honest. I feel sick to my stomach just thinking about it.

Her cell phone rang, and she saw Julio's name on the screen. "Yes, Julio. What is it?"

"The doctor just called with the results of the test concerning Ana's stomach problems. Baby, it's not good. She needs surgery, and it's going to cost around $40,000. He said it's not an uncommon condition among children who are born to mothers who are addicted to drugs."

Rosa sat down in shock. They didn't have that kind of money, and they didn't even know where their daughter, Ana's mother, was, and even if they did know, Ana's mother probably wouldn't care. She sure hadn't expressed any concern about her children when she'd left.

She heard Julio say, "Baby, are you there?"

"Yes, I'm here. I just don't know what we can do. Did the doctor say what would happen if Ana didn't have the operation?"

"Yeah, I asked the same question. He said if Ana doesn't have the surgery, she would continue to vomit and have diarrhea and ultimately it could result in her death. Baby, remember last night when you told me about the man who offered you money to turn off the security system at Mrs. Jensen's home when you left for the evening? We could sure use that money to pay for Ana's surgery. I don't think we can get it anywhere else. I know how much you don't want to do it, but Rosa, we don't have a choice. It's the money or our granddaughter's life, and I don't think either one of us wants to feel guilty for the rest of our lives because we didn't take money that could have saved her life and allowed her to lead a normal life. What do you think?"

Rosa was quiet for a long time. "Julio, I suppose you're right. I couldn't live with myself if that child died and I hadn't done something to save her life when I had the chance. I'll call him now. Why don't you call the doctor back and schedule the surgery."

A few moments later Rosa heard a voice, say, "This is Lou."

"Lou, this is Rosa, Mrs. Jensen's housekeeper. When do you want me to leave the security system off, and when will I get the money?"

"I'll hand you the money this evening when you're waiting for the bus after you finish work. I'll park at the curb near the bus stop and wave to you. You wave back like I'm an old friend and walk over to the car. My window will be rolled down. Hold onto your purse and leave it open, putting it just inside the window. I'll place the envelope with the money inside it. I'll let you know when I want you to leave the system unarmed. See you later."

Just as Rosa ended the call, her stomach churning, Mrs. Jensen walked through the kitchen door from the garage. "Rosa, do you feel all right? You're white as a ghost."

"I'm fine, Mrs. Jensen. Julio just called and told me one of his relatives had passed away unexpectedly. It was quite a shock."

"Do you want to go home? I can certainly do without you the rest of the afternoon."

"Thank you, but I'm fine, really. I need to go upstairs and finish the bedrooms. Is there anything else you want me to do today?"

"No. George Ellis is taking me out to dinner tonight, so I won't be home this evening. If I think of anything, I'm sure it can wait until tomorrow."

Rosa walked up the stairs with wooden legs, not sure if she would be able to reach the next step. Each one seemed insurmountable to her. She silently cursed the gods that had allowed her to be put in a position like this. Mrs. Jensen was the best employer she had ever had and she, Rosa, was going to be responsible for Mrs. Jensen's favorite pieces of Meissen being stolen. Sometimes life didn't seem fair.

Of course I could think of it another way. If Lou hadn't approached me yesterday, I wouldn't have been able to tell Julio to go ahead with the surgery, and Ana might have died. I've heard of no-win situations, and I think I'm right in the middle of one.

CHAPTER FIVE

Late that afternoon Lou pulled over to the curb not far from the bus stop where Rosa was sitting and waved to her. She nonchalantly walked over to his car as if picking up an envelope with $45,000 in it was something she did every day.

"Rosa, I'll call you in a day or so, but here's one thing you need to know. Don't even think about double-crossing me. Bad things happen to granddaughters when their grandmother doesn't keep her word. We have a deal. When you take this $45,000, you are agreeing you will tell no one, and I mean no one, not the police or anyone else about our deal. You don't know me, and you never saw me. I don't want to have to be responsible for causing injury or death to someone in your family. Do you understand what I'm saying?"

She removed her purse from the car and slung the strap over her shoulder. "Yes, I understand. You don't need to worry. I'm so ashamed of what I'm doing I wouldn't want anyone to know about it," she said tearfully. Rosa turned away from his car, walked back to the bus stop, and sat down on the bench to wait for the bus. Lou eased his car back into traffic.

Naturally Lou Powell wasn't his real name. He'd been involved in the murky world of crime for a long time, and one of the first things anyone did when they became a player in that arena was to use an alias, or two, or three. Sometimes he wore a beard, other times he shaved his head. He had different colored contact lenses and fake mustaches and had become a master at reinventing himself. Many years ago he'd discovered how much collectors of art and antiques were willing to pay in order to complete a collection or own a certain piece of art they coveted. From that time on, he'd become a specialist in stealing pieces of art from an owner and selling it to a desperate buyer so they could get what he or she wanted. He often thought how much easier this type of crime was than the small crimes he'd committed for years that barely left him enough to survive on.

When I decided to specialize in stolen art and antiques, it was the best decision I ever made. The buyers will pay practically anything to own some art object they're determined to have, and there's always someone close to the owner who's desperate for money and finds a way for me to have access to it so I can steal it. If I have a willing buyer, I can find the piece they want, and I can also find a way to get it. It's really not all that difficult.

The buyers he was dealing with were almost always collectors who never intended for their collections to be featured in a magazine or on a television show. It was enough for them to simply possess the item. There was no way they would jeopardize having an item they had coveted be confiscated as evidence by the police. Their lips were sealed. Lou only took cash and always got it. A great deal of it. It had allowed him to buy a condominium on Seven Mile Beach on the western end of Grand Cayman Island. He also had an offshore bank account there so he could keep his money out of the United States and safe from the eyes of the IRS.

One of the things that had been critical to Lou's success was being able to find out who collected what and what pieces they desperately wanted for their collections. He attended auctions regularly and frequented the galleries in New York, Los Angeles, and San Francisco. Occasionally it involved him being in a foreign country to get what his client needed. It was a small world where gossip reigned as king. Identifying the collectors who had "pickers" looking for pieces at the different auctions had made it that much easier. Over time he'd learned there was a collector for everything, and they would pay astronomical figures to complete their collections and feed their egos. It was simply a matter of finding out who wanted what and then locating the what. He didn't like to dwell on the collateral damage that had sometimes occurred over the years when he'd matched up buyers with the objects they coveted. He regarded it as a necessary part of his profession.

Occasionally he'd found it necessary to injure someone when he was stealing the objects he needed. Once it had even resulted in death. No one would ever link the brown-eyed mustached intruder who had to shoot the owner of the netsuke collection with the grey-haired, blue-eyed man who walked with a limp and relied on a cane. The intricate netsuke ivory carvings from Japan were safe in the hands of the buyer by the time Lou boarded the plane for Grand Cayman. Unfortunately, the owner of the netsuke collection hadn't been quite as lucky. He'd died three days later in the hospital after his maid had found him the morning following the theft.

I really don't see a problem with this one. As soon as I get the pieces I'll contact Henry Siegelman about them. From everything I've heard, he'll pay whatever I ask for them. The maid, Rosa, will turn off the alarm system, and I'll go into the house, grab the Meissen Monkey Band set and be on my way. I'll sell the pieces of the set that Siegelman doesn't want to other buyers, so it won't look like he had anything to do with it.

According to my research, Pam Jensen spends almost every evening with the man who was a partner in her late husband's restaurant, Mai Tai Mama's. I'll be in and out before they even get back from dinner. She can collect the insurance on the stolen pieces, and in a day or so I'll be on my way to Grand Cayman. Win-win for everyone. Devan, my brown-skinned Cayman Island beauty, will be waiting for me with an island drink and that glorious body I'll lose myself in for the next couple of weeks. Yeah, time to get this one over with. Grand Cayman is calling to me.

CHAPTER SIX

George Ellis, the owner of Mai Tai Mama's, and the former business partner of Brian Jensen, drove his silver BMW the short distance to Pam Jensen's home and parked in the driveway. Brian had been deceased for several months, and George had treated Pam to dinner a number of times.

He remembered the first time he'd met Pam, which also happened to be the same date he'd fallen in love with her. Brian had brought her into the restaurant to introduce her to George. He was stunned by her beauty and charm. She was short with ash blond hair which had been professionally highlighted. The skin around her eyes crinkled when she smiled, making her large grey eyes seem even larger. Her complexion was flawless, and her hourglass figure spoke to hours spent in the gym. George couldn't believe the jealous feelings that immediately overwhelmed him– jealous that his partner was going to marry this beautiful prize of a woman.

I wonder if she has any idea how I feel about her. No, actually how I've felt about her all these years. She asked me once why I'd never married. I answered by telling her I'd never found the right woman. That wasn't quite true. I'd found the right woman I wanted to marry, but there was a little problem. She was married to my business partner and best friend. Sounds like some sleazy romance book. Sure, there were a lot of women over the years. People always kidded me about my "flavor of the month," but they didn't know that there had only been one woman for me from the moment I met her. Pam. I never even considered marrying anyone else.

He thought about the ring he had in his pocket. At their age, what was the point of waiting? Although she'd never given him a reason to think she'd marry him, on the other hand she'd never not given him a reason. He'd respected her too much to try and take the relationship beyond a kiss on the cheek when he took her home after one of their regular dinner dates. He opened his car door, feeling the butterfly wings in his stomach fluttering against each other.

No matter how many times he visited the Jensen home located in an affluent area of Palm Springs, he still marveled at the difference between the outside and the inside of the home. While the inside of the house was filled with Pam's antiques including her renowned 18th century Meissen china collection, the outside of the white block style house was pure mid-20th century desert style. Its U-shape surrounded a large courtyard which was filled with pots and brightly colored flowering plants hanging in baskets from a large tree in the center of the courtyard. A gate led into the courtyard, and he could see the desert hills behind the house, turning to gorgeous shades of mauves and pinks at this time of early evening. While the infinity pool and pool house weren't visible from the street, the overall effect of the house was understated desert elegance at its best.

This could end up to be the best night of my life or the worst, he thought wryly. *Well, I'll know one way or another in a few hours.* He rang the doorbell, and the door was immediately opened by Pam.

"You are so prompt, George, far more so than Brian, and I love it. It used to drive me nuts waiting for him to always do just one more thing," she said walking out the door and pulling it closed behind her. "Oops, I forget to set the alarm. Just be a sec." She unlocked the door and walked back into the house, returning a minute later.

"Don't you get tired of trying to remember to turn that thing on and off?" George asked as he steered his car towards Mai Tai Mama's. "That's why I bought a German shepherd. I tried a security system for a while, but I never could remember the code, and the Palm Springs police paid me more than one visit. Eventually they started sending me bills when my security system alerted them there was a problem only to find out it was a false alarm."

"No," she said, "I just use my birthday, 5-30-60. That makes it simple."

"Isn't that kind of a common thing to do? I remember reading somewhere that birthdays and pets' names are the most frequently used security codes and passwords. If someone knew your birthdate, they could easily disarm the system and gain access to your home."

"Oh George, quit being such a worry wart. Other than my children and now you, I don't think many people know my birthdate, and I rather doubt if either one of my children even remembers it."

"Pam, I worry about you living alone in that big house. Plus, you've got some pretty valuable paintings and antiques. I'd feel much better if you'd let me give you a trained guard dog."

"Thanks, but no thanks. I've thought about it and decided not to. My security system works just fine, and I don't want to even think what one swipe of a dog's tail could do to some of my antiques, like the glass paperweight collection on the coffee table. No, I think I'll just continue to use my birthdate."

"Well, the offer holds. Let me know if you change your mind. Wow, I love to see lots of cars already here at the restaurant. Looks like it's going to be a good night for Mai Tai Mama's. I know you've eaten here more times than you can count, but I still think we have the best food in Palm Springs. Hope you don't mind."

"Are you kidding? Where else can I go that they know exactly how I like my steak cooked, that I like a salad very lightly dressed with just three croutons, and that I prefer chives on my baked potato rather than the standard green onions. And I can't forget about the bottles of Silver Oak cabernet sauvignon below the bar they keep primarily for me. No, George, you never need to apologize for bringing me here. I'm just glad Brian sold you his share of the restaurant rather than willing it to me. I love eating here, but I never had any desire to try and run it. You do a very good job."

"Thanks." As soon as the hostess saw George she stepped out from behind the host stand and guided them to their table. It never varied – it was the corner table in the main room so George could wave to people and keep an eye on what was happening in the restaurant.

Pam always ordered the same thing every time she came to the restaurant, a pan fried rib eye steak medium rare with a wine and mushroom reduction sauce. Years ago she'd gotten the recipe from the chef, and she'd often made it for Brian on special occasions. Since his death she hadn't felt like making it for just herself, but whenever she came to Mai Tai Mama's that was what she ordered, and she was never disappointed.

"George, I'm so glad this is still on the menu. I know with the name of the restaurant you and Brian put a lot of Asian dishes on the menu, but there are a lot of people like me who still love a good steak, and this sauce makes it. Even after all these years, it's still my favorite thing to eat. Thanks."

Dinner was superb as always, but when the present owner and the past half-owner's wife were the diners, that might have had something to do with the food and the service. Pam and George had known each other for over twenty-five years and had shared a lot of each other's lives, so the conversation between the two of them was always easy and periods of silence were rare. Tonight was an exception. George seemed ill-at-ease, and finally Pam felt she had to say something.

"George, is anything wrong? You seem distracted and quite unlike your normal self. Want to tell me about it?"

He swallowed several times, looked around, and began to speak. "Pam, this is harder than I thought it would be. You see, I've been in love with you from the moment Brian brought you to the restaurant to meet me. That's why I never got married." He stopped and took a drink of water. "Pam, I want to marry you. I know Brian has only been gone a few months, but at our age I don't see much of a reason to wait." George reached into his jacket pocket and took out a small velvet box. He opened it, revealing a large diamond solitaire engagement ring. "Pam, will you marry me?"

Pam looked at him in horror. Her mouth was dry, and she felt like she was watching a scene from a bad movie. Finally she spoke. "George, I consider you to be one of my closest friends, but I'm sorry, that's all it is, friendship. I don't love you, and I never will. Brian was the only man I ever loved, and I have no plans to ever marry again. If I let you think otherwise, I'm truly sorry. I'd like to forget this whole conversation ever happened and go back to the way we were. If what I'm saying causes you pain, I am so sorry."

George's face was ashen as he stood up and called the waiter over. "Tell the valet to bring my car around." He strode out of the restaurant with Pam trying to keep up with him.

When he hadn't spoken for several minutes on the way home, Pam said, "George, I apologize again if I ever gave you cause to think our relationship would turn into something else. I'm truly sorry. Please, tell me we can go back to the way it was."

He turned and looked at her. "For the last twenty-five years I've wanted you, and when Brian died I thought I could finally have you as my wife. Obviously from what you said earlier, I was wrong. Given that, I don't think we can remain friends any longer. After tonight I never want to see you again," he said as he pulled into her driveway. She looked at him and opened the car door, realizing he wasn't going to get out of the car and open it for her.

"Goodnight George. I wish you the best, I really do, and I'm very, very sorry if I've hurt you." She closed the door and walked up the walkway to her home. A moment later George threw the car in reverse, reached the street and accelerated as fast as he could. All he wanted to do was put as much distance as he could between Pam Jensen and himself.

I can't believe this. This is a nightmare. I thought she'd take the ring and we'd get married. That's what I've wanted and thought would happen all these years. Now it's over. I really don't have anything to live for. I might as well be dead.

Slowly his sense of disbelief gave way to an intense feeling of rage. His cheeks became hot and a ball of fury started to burn in his stomach. George still couldn't believe what she had just told him.

Nobody does this to George Ellis, not after I've put my life on hold for her. I'd rather see her dead than with someone else. Maybe that's what I'll do, kill her. That way, if I can't have her, no one else will either.

The code on Pam's security system popped into his mind, and he began to consider how he would take his revenge out on Pam Jensen. For the first time in almost an hour, he smiled as a plan began to form in his mind.

CHAPTER SEVEN

There was a soft knock on Marty's door the next morning, and she heard her sister saying, "Marty, it's time. We'd better get going, or we'll be late."

Marty picked up her keys, gave Duke a pat on the head, and walked out the door. "Let's take my car," Marty said, "I can write it off."

"Not much to write off. It's only a thirty minute drive to town," Laura said, "but that's fine with me. I drive enough as it is. Do you realize in all these years I've never been on an appraisal with you? I'm excited about it. Do you have everything you need?"

"Yes. I'm pretty sure I do," Marty said. "The most important thing is my magnifying glass. I've got a really good one that's incorporated into a beautiful piece of jewelry. Years ago, while we were still married, Scott gave me a magnifying glass set in gold with little diamonds around it and attached it to a long heavy gold chain which I wear around my neck. It's a beautiful piece of jewelry, even if he did give it to me, but it's also very functional. I have my camera, my tape recorder, a pad of paper, a pen, and a tape measure, all the things I'll need to do the appraisal."

"So what specifically will you do?" Laura asked.

"Well, first of all I'll go from room to room to get a general idea what's in the home. With antique and art items, I'll photograph each item, measure it, dictate what it looks like, look for specific identifiable marks, and things of that nature. You'll also see me do some other things such as running my finger around the rim of a glass or art glass piece. Often the eye won't see a chip or a nick, but the finger will feel it, and it really diminishes the value. I do the same thing with cut glass items. Items that look like cut glass but are knock-offs have a different feel than those that are true cut glass. That's the type of stuff you learn after years of appraising. I've never seen those kinds of tips in the books about how to appraise antique art objects. I've just picked them up over the years.

"Anyway, depending on what the client wants, in estate appraisals I usually lump the non-antique and art items into several groups such as appliances, kitchen items, towels, blankets, etcetera and assign a value to them. If the client wants each one individually appraised, it can increase the cost of the appraisal by thousands. I mean I'm not complaining if that's what the client wants, but it seems like a waste of money, and usually it's completely unnecessary.

"I remember one time I was doing an appraisal for the Resolution Trust Corporation when a lot of the savings and loan companies went bankrupt in the 1980's. I was appraising the items in a savings and loan branch office, and the only things that had any monetary value in a fair market value appraisal were the potted plants. I always felt a bit guilty about that appraisal. My fee was more than the value of all of the items in the building. There were over two dozen supposedly fine art paintings hanging on the walls of the building. In order to inflate the value of the savings and loan assets, they had placed the value of the paintings, on their books, at five hundred thousand dollars. They were actually cheap paper prints worth no more than two hundred dollars in total. I always wondered what the interior decorator had originally charged the savings and loan company."

"This is a whole new world to me," Laura said, "but I think I better tell you something. You know I have some psychic abilities that can't be explained. Well, last night I kept waking up with a bad feeling about this appraisal. I don't know what it was about or why I felt like I did. I kept getting a feeling that the murder of the woman was tied to something that's no longer in the house. Something you won't be able to appraise because it's not there. When I walk through the house with you, I might be prompted with some new thoughts, and it may be a little clearer. Would you like me to tell you what I feel or keep my mouth shut?"

Marty looked at her sister who was dressed in a chic dark blue pant suit with a cream shell under the jacket. In contrast to the turbans and heavy jewelry a lot of psychics wore, no one would ever look at the woman wearing small pearl earrings with a pearl barrette holding back her red hair and think, *This woman is a psychic.* There was absolutely nothing about Laura that would indicate she possessed certain unseen powers.

"I'm no detective, and I haven't been hired to do anything like that, but yes, even if it has nothing to do with my appraisal I'd like to know what you think or feel. Are your feelings always right? Who knows? Maybe you and I will end up solving the crime," she said laughing.

"Don't plan on it," Laura said. "I'm right more than I'm wrong, but sure, sometimes I'll get a feeling or a vision and nothing happens. By the way, you mentioned what was involved in appraising an item, but once you do the initial identification of the item, then what?"

"That's where the real appraising comes in, and I have to make some judgment calls. Silver, china, glassware, and a lot of furniture and other things I can take by myself from start to finish. In other words, I know enough to write up the identification and assign a fair market value to the item. I dictate an inventory list of those items, put a value on them, and send them along with my photographs to a woman who has done my transcriptions for years. She'll put it together for me in the proper report form and ship it to me for proofing. When it's ready to go to the client, I'll have a copy made for my file and send the original to the client. Sometimes an insurance company wants a copy as well."

"Sounds terribly complicated to me," Laura said.

"Trust me, it's not, but what it does require is years of experience. What I didn't mention is how I appraise things when I don't consider myself qualified to appraise a particular item. In those situations I rely on the expertise of others who specialize in areas like pre-Columbian art, certain ethnic pieces, gun collections, knives, and other things that aren't within the normal antique and art appraiser's scope of knowledge.

"For instance, I'm not an expert in jewelry. I've made some contacts in Palm Springs with several jewelers, and I can take a photograph of the piece of jewelry, actually I usually take several photographs of the item, and show the jeweler what I have. They can usually give me a valuation based on the photograph. If someone has a lot of items in an area like jewelry or pre-Columbian art, it's worthwhile to hire an appraiser who has expertise in that area. Being a town with a lot of wealth, Palm Springs has a lot of appraisers who live and work here. I've made it a point to meet with the ones who aren't generalists like me, as well as some who specialize in what I do in case I have a job that needs more than one person.

"Well, looks like we're almost there, so I'll know what I'm dealing with in a few minutes." She turned into the driveway of a large white U-shaped mid-50's style home. "Wow! What a beautiful house," she said. "It's really in keeping with the desert. I wonder how she ever came to acquire and collect the things Dick mentioned. It seems so out of character with the feel of the desert. I could understand it more if she collected Native American rugs and baskets or some such thing."

"I don't know, but it looks like you'll be able to find out real soon. A large SUV just pulled in behind us. It's probably her son, and Marty, FYI, I'm getting bad vibes from him."

Marty stopped the car and turned and looked at Laura. "You're getting bad vibes, and you haven't even met him? How does that work?"

"I have no idea how any of this works, but I will tell you I not only have bad vibes about him, I also have bad vibes about this house."

"Swell. This should really be entertaining. Okay, let's do it."

CHAPTER EIGHT

At the same time that Laura and Marty got out of Marty's car, Jim Warren stepped out of his SUV. He walked over to them and said, "Hi, I'm Jim Warren. Which one of you is Marty Morgan?"

"That's me," Marty said. "It's nice to meet you. I'm sorry about your mother. I'm here to help you in any way I can. I understand that the appraisal is to be done for the purposes of probate."

"Yes, that's correct. I was concerned my stepsister was going to contest the Will, but so far she hasn't. My mother left everything to my sister and me. I have her Will, and as soon as her attorney gets back from his trip, he'll be filing it with the Court. How long do you think the appraisal will take?" he asked, pointedly looking at his watch.

"I have no idea since I don't know what antiques, art, and collectibles are in the house."

He unlocked the gate that led to the courtyard and the front door of the house. "Even though the gate's locked, my mother's housekeeper, Rosa, should be here. Mom instructed her to always keep the gate locked." He rang a bell. A few moments later the front door was opened by a small Hispanic woman with her greying hair pulled back off of her face and secured by a clip at the nape of her neck.

"Hello, Rosa. This is the appraiser I told you about." He looked at Marty and then at Laura.

"This is my sister, Laura. She works for Alliance Property and Casualty Company and agreed to act as my gofer. Often I need an assistant to hold a painting or some such thing, so I can photograph it. Rosa, I'm Marty Morgan. I'm the one doing the appraisal."

"Please come in. How can I help you?"

"At the moment I don't know." She turned to Jim. "I always begin my appraisals in probate situations with a walk through of the house to determine the scope of the appraisal. When I'm finished, I can give you an estimate of how much time I'll need to spend on the premises. Is that all right with you?"

"Of course. Let's start with the kitchen." They walked to the rear of the house where the kitchen and breakfast nook overlooked an infinity pool that looked as if it was going to flow off into the desert. Marty spent several minutes opening cabinets and looking in drawers.

"There are quite a few things in here which definitely are of value. Your mother evidently collected Quimper pottery. It looks like the pieces are from the 18th century and are highly desirable as well as expensive. The fifteen plates on this wall will all need to be individually appraised. There are some other pieces in the cabinets which definitely have value as does the sterling silver and chinaware. Those I will be appraising. As far as the run-of-the-mill kitchen items and appliances, I think it would be fine to lump them together as miscellaneous kitchen items, and I'll assign a value to the lot. Not appraising them piece by piece will save you quite a bit of money on the appraisal. If the Will is going to be contested, I'll have to do it piece by piece, but if not, there shouldn't be any problem in doing them in bulk."

"No, I don't think there will be a Will contest, but you never know. Just appraise those items in bulk. Go ahead and walk through the rest of the house. I'm going to spend a little time in my mother's study, and see if I can decipher some of the things in her desk."

For the next half hour Marty and Laura walked through each room of the house. Clearly, Pam Jensen had been very knowledgeable about antiques. There were collections of antique perfume bottles in the master bathroom, fine art on the walls throughout the house, antique furniture in all of the bedrooms and the dining room, a breakfront filled with cut glass, and a library with antique books spilling out of the floor to ceiling bookcases. Everywhere they looked it was a feast for the eyes.

"Laura, remember how I told you sometimes I needed to bring in an appraiser in a certain area when it wasn't within my scope of expertise. Well, you're looking at one of the areas now. There's a man in Palm Springs who specializes in antique books. I'm going to ask him to appraise these for me. What I do in a case like this is pay him directly and then attach his appraisal to mine."

The one room left was the living room. When they walked into it Marty caught her breath and stopped. "What's wrong?" Laura asked.

"The Meissen collection in this display case is quite simply the finest I've ever seen. Look at this room. It should be in a museum. Everything in here is worth a fortune from the mirrors with the rococo frames to the Aubusson tapestry on the wall to say nothing of the antique Oriental rugs casually scattered around on the floor. Not only did Pam Jensen have an excellent eye for antiques, she also had an ability few collectors possess – being able to blend different types of antiques in a pleasing way, so nothing jumps out, it just all becomes one cohesive unit. Wow! I've done a lot of appraisals over the years, but I've never seen this many fabulous items in one place."

Jim joined them in the living room. "Have you had a chance to get the lay of the land?" he asked.

"Yes. Your mother was obviously one of the most astute collectors I've ever encountered. Not only is her collection one of the finest I've ever seen, she had an ability to combine everything in a warm, welcoming way. As far as timing, I'm estimating three days to conduct the on-site appraisal, then additional time for research and preparation of the report. Antique books are not my forte, so I'll need to bring in another appraiser for them. Is there anything else I should know before I get started?"

"Yes. My mother had a lot of jewelry. Let me get it out of her safe and show you. Let's go into her bedroom." After the three of them walked to the bedroom, Jim knelt down, pulling the rug back which revealed a floor safe. He opened it and removed handfuls of jewelry.

Marty looked at the jewelry for a moment and said, "I'm going to have to call a friend of mine who's an expert in jewelry. I would be doing a disservice to you by appraising it. Just like the antique books, I'll attach his appraisal to the main appraisal."

"There's one other thing. My mother had a ten carat marquise cut diamond ring in a platinum setting that Brian gave her for their twentieth anniversary. It's not in the safe, and I can't find it. While you're appraising everything, I'd like you to keep an eye out for the ring. Here's my address. You can send me the appraisal when you've completed it."

"I should have it within a few weeks. I do require a retainer of three thousand dollars on an estate of this size with the rest due when I deliver my appraisal."

"No problem. I'll write a check out now." A moment later he handed her a check in the amount of three thousand dollars.

CHAPTER NINE

"Let's start in the kitchen," Marty said after they'd said goodbye to Jim. "I like to do my appraisals by going room by room. When I'm finished with a room, I do one more walk around in it and then put that room and what I've appraised in it out of my mind and get ready for the next one. May seem silly, but it works for me. I know some appraisers do it by category. In other words, they'll do all the rugs in the house at the same time, or all the glassware. There are no hard and fast rules on how to conduct an appraisal, but my method works best for me."

"What do you want me to do?" Laura asked.

"I'd like you to take those Quimper plates off the wall, one at a time, and bring each one over to me. When I've recorded the necessary information and photographed it, you can put it back exactly where it was."

Rosa walked into the kitchen. "Is there anything I can do to help you?" she asked.

"Not a thing. We'll probably be in the kitchen for the next couple of hours, and then I'll start on the dining room."

"Let me make you some lunch. Mrs. Jensen loved my Mexican Eggs Benedict, and I can prepare them for you when you're finished in the kitchen. It would make me feel like I'm doing something for her."

"Thank you. That would be lovely. If we don't have to stop and leave for lunch, the appraisal will go faster. I'll let you know when we finish up in here."

When Rosa was out of earshot, Laura leaned over to Marty at the table where she was setting up and said, "You asked me to let you know what I felt, so here's the first thing. Rosa is definitely spooked by something. I don't get the feeling that she murdered Mrs. Jensen, but she knows something, and I'm getting a real feeling of guilt from her."

"Okay, good to know. I'll keep it in mind. Let's get on with this. Start with the top plate, left hand side. Go across that row and then back to the left middle row, etcetera."

"What makes these so valuable, Marty?" Laura asked as she placed a plate which displayed a brightly colored French peasant woman on it in front of Marty. "I mean, they have a certain charm, but why do you suppose she collected these?"

"From what I'm seeing, she only collected the best. From our quick walkthrough and looking at these plates, there's not a nick or scratch on them, which is highly unusual when you're dealing with tin glazed pottery. Obviously they're French, and the marks are telling me they were made in the early 18th century, which makes them some of the earliest around. To have them be that old and not damaged means they're worth a lot of money. Quimper pottery was made in all kinds of forms, from knife rests to inkstands to figurines, and about everything else. They usually had designs of Breton peasants, animals, flowers, or sea forms. These plates are the best I've run across."

"Would I be right in assuming she didn't eat off of these plates?"

"I would be highly doubtful. Lead was often used in the glaze of early pottery pieces. In the early 20th century a leadless glaze was developed, but there's always been talk that early pottery pieces could be dangerous to anyone who ate off of them. They were primarily decorative items."

Two hours later, after Laura had counted all of the kitchenware items and sorted them, and Marty had photographed everything and taken the information she needed from the antique items, Marty said, "Time to tell Rosa we could use some lunch. Don't know about you, but I'm hungry, and I need a break." She walked out of the kitchen and said in a loud voice, "Rosa, I think we're ready for lunch. Thank you so much. We'll be in the dining room."

Rosa appeared from the bathroom with cleaning items in a basket and said, "Perfect timing. I just finished cleaning the bathroom. Lunch will be ready in about twenty minutes. Would iced tea be all right with you?"

"Sounds wonderful. Thank you."

"Laura, trust me, I doubt if you'll ever see antiques like this in any home. I venture to say this collection is probably the best your insurance company insures. I mean, a whole room full of Chippendale and Hepplewhite furniture? Impossible! You see some in museums, but this is incredible. I don't know if she had a budget or what, but somebody was major bucks up, and I mean major, if they could buy these items. Here, you could hold this end of the tape measure for me."

Twenty minutes later Rosa walked into the dining room, "Lunch is ready. I think it's too warm out to eat on the patio, so I set the table in the breakfast nook. It has a nice view of the infinity pool and the hills. I hope that's all right."

"Definitely. We could both use a break. Thank you," Marty said as they followed Rosa into the kitchen. "I've never had Mexican Eggs Benedict before, but from the way they look, I'm probably going to want the recipe."

"I'd be happy to give it you. My mother often made it on Sundays when we returned from Mass. Please enjoy."

"That's exactly what I intend to do," Marty said, taking a forkful of egg and cornbread. After a moment, she looked over at the sink where Rosa was washing the dishes she'd used in making the luncheon. "Rosa, this is fabulous. I definitely want the recipe."

"Thank you. Were you expecting anyone? The gate buzzer just rang."

"No. Go ahead and answer it. We're fine."

As soon as she was gone, Laura whispered, "Sorry, Marty, you may not want to hear this, but I can see Rosa' aura and it's black, which would fit in with the guilty feeling I was getting earlier. She definitely knows something and may have even had something to do with the murder, and if she didn't, she's afraid she did."

"Laura, come on. How can you know that? You're going to tell me that sweet little woman had something to do with the woman who was murdered, the woman who had employed her for years? I don't buy it."

"Quite frankly, I don't care whether you buy it or not. I'm simply telling you what I'm seeing."

"Let's just drop it for now. I want to enjoy this meal. Actually we should probably tell John about it. I'll bet The Red Pony could sell this pretty easily. He could make the cornbread ahead of time like Rosa did and then just heat the beans, poach the eggs, and put on the finishing touches. Gotta give him the recipe tonight. I'll get it from Rosa before we leave."

Rosa walked back into the kitchen accompanied by a large heavyset man with greying hair and a mustache to match. Marty had no idea who he was, but he certainly looked like someone she would definitely like to get to know better.

CHAPTER TEN

As Marty looked up from her plate of Mexican Eggs Benedict at the big handsome man who had just walked into the room she felt her heart do a flip-flop. For absolutely no reason whatsoever she had the fleeting thought, *so you've come, I've been waiting for you. Huh? What is this all about? What is going on? I feel like a teenager. I can barely look at him, he's so gorgeous. It must have something to do with Laura's psychic powers. I'll get back at her later.*

The big man said, "Hi, I'm Detective Jeff Combs with the Palm Springs Police Department. Which one of you is Marty?"

"That would be me," she said in a strained voice. It was all she could do to get it out of her mouth. She was completely flustered by him and hoped she didn't faint or do something else equally unsophisticated.

"Well, Marty it's nice to meet you. And this must be your sister, Laura. Would I be correct?"

"That you would," Laura said. "Why don't you sit down and join us? We were just finishing lunch. I'm sure Rosa has more makings for the Mexican Eggs Benedict and can poach some eggs quickly."

"I'd love to join you, but I just ate lunch, however I would take a glass of iced tea," he said, turning to Rosa, "if that's not too much trouble."

Rosa placed a frosty glass of iced tea in front of him and walked back to the sink to finish the dishes she'd been washing.

"When Jim told me he was having the items appraised I thought I'd better meet the appraiser and ask a few questions since this is a murder investigation, and you might find something out that could be important concerning the case."

"Marty, I'll be back in a minute. I need to use the bathroom," Laura said.

When she was gone, Marty turned to the detective and said, "Of course. What kind of questions can I answer for you?"

"Well, first of all I see you're not wearing a wedding ring. May I assume you're not married?"

"Yes," Marty said, feeling her face redden, "but what does that have to do with my appraisal?"

"Absolutely nothing, but I wanted to find out. I don't know if you're aware of it, actually I don't see how you couldn't be, but I feel like there's some kind of an electric spark going back and forth between us. If I'm really out of line, I apologize. This is crazy."

"I agree, it's crazy. Let's get back to the appraisal," she said hoping he didn't see the twitch in her right eyelid which always happened when she got nervous.

"Marty, are you okay?" Jeff said, leaning towards her. "It looks like your right eyelid is twitching."

"Yes, I'm fine. It happens sometimes when I'm tired. I've really been concentrating this morning. I'm sure that's what it is. It's nothing to be concerned about."

Laura walked back into the room, took one look at Marty and said, "Marty, what's wrong? Your eyelid's twitching, and it only twitches when you're nervous."

When we get in the car and drive back to the compound, I am going to stop the car, throw you out, and make you walk back the rest of the way. Let's see if your psychic stuff picks up on that. Maybe it will teach you to keep your big mouth shut.

"No, I'm not nervous at all," Marty said. "Probably just a little tired from how hard I was concentrating this morning." She turned to the detective. "How can I help you?"

"You know that Mrs. Jensen was murdered last week. I just got the coroner's report, and it indicates that the murder weapon was a .9mm pistol. The bullet was lodged in her chest. What I would ask of you is if you see anything you think is strange or something you think I might want to know, please tell me."

"Of course. What kinds of things should I be looking for?" Marty asked.

"Obviously if you find a gun I want to know about it. I don't know much about antiques. That's your field. I'm curious if she had some antiques other collectors would want, maybe even kill for."

"I haven't run across any yet, but this is just the first day of the appraisal."

"Her son, Jim, tells me he and his sister are going to inherit everything according to the terms of the Will, and he also mentioned he hadn't been able to find a ten carat diamond ring his mother owned. He said he'd asked you to keep an eye out for it." He smiled at her, and she felt her heart flipping around in her chest like a trout trying to jump out of the net. The thought brought back a memory of her father fishing with her when she was young. Her job had been to put the net in the water so her father could get the trout in it.

Keep it together, Marty, keep it together. You can fall apart when you get home tonight. He's got to be leaving soon.

"Yes, he mentioned that to me and of course, I'll keep an eye out for it. Do you have any suspects at the moment?"

"No, and that's very frustrating. Her husband's deceased, she seemed to have a good relationship with her children, and no one has told me anything scandalous about her, and yet someone wanted her dead. Cases like this one are what's causing my hair to prematurely turn grey."

"I can imagine. I'll let you know if I find anything."

"Here's my business card, and I'll write my cell phone number on the back. I'd like your number as well in case I need to get in touch with you. Actually, let me have your address too. Sometimes cell phones don't work in the hills," Jeff said with a roguish grin. He watched while she entered his number in the contacts list on her cell phone.

At the sound of the gate buzzer, Rosa turned to the detective and said, "Are you expecting someone?"

"No. my staff doesn't even know I'm here. What's the buzzer for?"

"It's the front gate. I'll answer it and see who it is."

CHAPTER ELEVEN

Rosa walked over to the intercom and said, "Who is it?"

"Rosa, it's Nikki Bolen. Could I come in for a minute?"

"She was Mrs. Jensen's best friend. Is it all right if I buzz her in?" Rosa asked, her hand covering the intercom. All three of them nodded in the affirmative. "I'm unlocking the gate right now, Mrs. Bolen. I'll meet you at the front door."

A few moments later a beautiful dark haired woman entered the kitchen. "Hi, I'm Nikki Bolen. I was probably Pam's best friend," she said, extending a well-tended hand to them. She was dressed in a simple white blouse and khaki skirt with white wedged sandals in stark contrast to her perfectly polished red toenails. Although there was nothing ostentatious about her outfit, Marty knew she was looking at a woman who was wearing about $1,000 worth of clothes to say nothing of the enormous diamond ring on her ring finger. Although the diamond ring far surpassed the diamond tennis bracelet and the diamond stud earrings she wore, and even though jewelry wasn't her specialty and she usually had to get an expert's opinion on the value of it, Marty knew Nikki's jewelry alone was worth thousands of dollars.

"May I join you? Rosa, if you wouldn't mind, that iced tea looks so good, I'd love a glass. Detective, it's good to see you again. Have you found out anything about Pam's death?"

"Nikki, I wish I could tell you we'd arrested whoever did it, but unfortunately at this moment I don't even have a suspect. You were her closest friend. Maybe you can tell me something that will help. Actually, I was going to call you to see if you had any ideas."

"Well, Detective, feel free to call me any time," she said, batting her eyelashes at him.

Marty felt a sudden white hot flash of hatred for the woman. *What in the devil is wrong with me? It's obvious they know each other. I'm the new kid on the block. For all I know they may have been involved in a relationship for years. This is absolutely crazy. I've got to get ahold of myself.*

"What can you tell me about Mrs. Jensen? I know she was wealthy and quite beautiful, but in a town like Palm Springs, that doesn't make her all that different from a lot of other women," the detective said, a little nervously Marty thought.

"Pam had three passions in life. First was Brian. She was devastated when he died, even though he was fifteen years older than she was. Her other two passions were non-profit organizations and her antique collection. She was on the board of most of the major charitable organizations in the city and gave to almost every cause, from stray cats to runaway children to the homeless. When she married Brian, she was immediately admitted into a very rarified group – the extremely wealthy people of Palm Springs. Because she knew these people, she was very effective at raising money for her favorite charities."

"From what I've seen this morning, she also must have spent a great deal of time learning about antiques and following auctions," Marty said.

"Yes, that was her third passion. She often bid by phone when major auction houses throughout the United States, actually all over the world, had a piece she wanted. She was very knowledgeable, and I've been with her on a number of occasions when she was bidding.

She knew exactly when to stop and never got caught up in the hype and almost circus like atmosphere that often surrounded the items."

"Was she emotionally attached to the items, or did she collect mainly for investment purposes?" Marty asked, "Not that it makes any difference in the valuation of the pieces."

"She was emotionally attached in that she enjoyed everything she bought. There were some jewelry pieces she loved, and certainly she loved the Meissen Monkey Band. I think the rest of her antiques simply brought joy to her. Even though Pam had an outstanding collection, I never heard her brag about it. In fact, people often brought the subject of her collection up in a conversation with her, because they had heard how extraordinary it was.

"Turning to another subject, Pam's husband felt her son, Jim, was trying to bleed her dry, and I don't know if you know this, but Pam told me last week that she'd mentioned to Jim she was going to have a new Will prepared. From what she told me, he was furious. She was afraid she'd lose her courage, so she went to her lawyer and did it."

"Do you know why Jim was so angry and what was in the new Will? This might be very important to the case," Jeff asked.

"She felt very bad that Brian had left his daughter by his first marriage, Amy, out of his Will. Pam never felt very good about taking Amy's father from her and developed a very good relationship with her. They often saw each other, and I know Pam was very fond of her. Pam knew that Brian would disapprove of the relationship, so she never told him about it. After he died and left everything to her, Pam decided to add Amy to her Will. She willed half of her estate to Amy and the other half to her son and daughter, Jim and Marilyn."

"Wow, that means Jim would lose half of his inheritance when that happened. Right?" Laura asked.

"Yes. I know she did it because we met for lunch afterwards, and she was a little shaken up about it, because she knew Jim would probably be furious that she'd actually done it." She turned to

Detective Combs. "Do you know if Jim has found out about it?"

Marty spoke up. "I don't think he knows about the change in her Will, because he told me he and his sister were the sole beneficiaries. Nothing was said about Amy."

"We talked about suspects earlier," Jeff said, "and I said we had none. I think I have one now if Jim found out his mother had, in fact, changed her Will. When I talked to Jim, he gave me the name of Pam's attorney, and I called his office. He's out of town, but he's due back this afternoon. I asked his secretary to call me when he returns."

"I have a nail appointment," Nikki said, looking at her watch. "I really need to go. Nice to meet you," she said to Marty and Laura. She turned to Jeff, "You already have my phone number. I'd love to hear from you. Rosa, would you lock the door behind me?" She turned and walked out the kitchen and towards the front door. Within seconds they heard her scream.

Jeff jumped up and ran to where Nikki stood pointing her finger at the Meissen collection, Rosa not far behind her. Laura and Marty joined them. "Nikki, what's wrong?" She was absolutely white, and her hand was shaking.

"The Monkey Band is gone."

"I'm sorry, Nikki, I have no idea what you're talking about," Jeff said.

"Remember, I told you it was one of the few antiques that Pam was attached to. It was her pride and joy. Brian bought it for her, and there are very few complete and original sets like hers in the world. The set dated from the 18th century and was almost priceless. It looks like the rest of the Meissen collection is here." She turned to Jeff and said, "Pam told me once that people would kill to own the Monkey Band. It was that rare. If you find out who wanted the Monkey Band, you'll probably have another suspect." She turned and walked out the door.

"Rosa, what can you tell me about this? Do you know anything about it being missing?"

"No. I dusted her Meissen collection about once a week, sometimes less than that because it was behind glass and didn't collect much dust. It was here the last time I dusted."

Marty noticed that Laura was staring intently at Rosa and knew she'd hear more about that later.

Just then Jeff's phone rang. "Yes, I'm on my way," he said. "Ladies, I've enjoyed talking to you. Marty I'll probably call you this evening to find out more about this Monkey Band thing. Right now I'm needed down at the station. Rosa, thank you for the iced tea." He hurriedly walked out the front door.

CHAPTER TWELVE

After Nikki and Jeff had left, Marty turned to Laura and said, "Back to work. We need to finish up the dining room. That's going to take some time because the antiques in there are really superb, and they need to be fully documented. Rosa, we'll be in the dining room if you need us."

When Rosa was safely out of earshot, Laura said, "Did you notice how nervous Rosa was when Nikki screamed that the Monkey Band was missing? Honestly, she turned pale and her hand involuntarily went to her heart. That's usually a tell - or that's what us psychics call it when someone does something involuntarily, and it's very revealing. It's a subconscious thing people don't even know they're doing, and it indicates they're nervous or scared or know more than they're telling about something."

"I was so busy looking to see what Nikki was so upset about that I wasn't paying attention to Rosa. We can talk about it tonight."

"Sure, if you'll tell me what's up with you and the handsome detective. Wow, what a hunk he is! And if you don't mind me saying so, good sister of mine, I think he's really interested in you."

"Laura, absolutely nothing is up between the two of us. We'll just probably be seeing more of him because he's the detective assigned to the case."

"Right," Laura said grinning mischievously. "Okay, I won't harass you about him and the look he gave you, but you could sure do a lot worse."

"For your information, I am not interested in any men at the present time, and that certainly includes Detective Combs. Now hold the tape measure, so I can get some accurate measurements. By the way, remind me I need to call Carl Mitchell and the antique book guy whose name I can't remember when we get home. Carl owns an antique shop in downtown Palm Springs, and is very knowledgeable about almost all antiques, but his real expertise is jewelry, and from what I saw when Jim took the jewelry out of the safe in his mother's bedroom, those pieces need to be examined by an expert. I could probably do it myself, but in an appraisal like this one, I'd be doing a disservice not to have them examined by Carl. Since the Will may be contested, it's even more critical to cross all the t's and dot the i's."

The remainder of the afternoon was spent appraising items in the dining room and two of the three bathrooms in the house. Even though there weren't extensive collections in either of the bathrooms, antique mirrors and other decorative objects had to be appraised.

At 4:30, Marty turned to Laura and said, "I'm brain dead. All I want to do is go home, pet Duke, and have a glass of wine. Let's find Rosa and tell her we'll see her in the morning."

"Can we leave all your equipment here, or do we need to take it with us?"

"It would be a lot easier if we left it here, but I want to look at the photos I took and make sure they all came out okay. I also took a lot of photos of the jewelry, ones I want to send to Carl to give him a broad overview of what's here. Usually when I have him join me in an appraisal, we meet before his shop opens at ten."

"How long do you think it will take him?" Laura asked. "I guess I'm asking what time we need to be here in the morning."

"I think I'll make an appointment to meet with him here at the house at eight in the morning. That will give him almost an hour and forty-five minutes to do the appraisal, and he can get back to his shop in time to open. That should be plenty of time. I can help him by taking the types of photos he'll need for the appraisal. If he can meet with us at eight, I'll call Rosa. The other alternative is for him to come to the house after his shop closes."

Twenty minutes later on their drive back to the compound, Laura looked out the window and said, "There's the compound in the distance. It always makes me happy to come home to it. I still can't believe I ever found it, and it was for sale. It sure was my lucky day. It's so perfect. Les says he's done his best art work ever since he started living here."

"I like him, but I don't recall you ever telling me how you met him," Marty said.

"One of Alliance's insureds is an art gallery. Dick thought we should be represented at the grand opening of their second gallery. The artist they were showcasing was Les. I attended the grand opening as a representative of Alliance, and that's where I met Les. That was over five years ago. We have a wonderful relationship, and I still pinch myself every day to make sure it's really me he's interested in."

"You sell yourself short," Marty said. "What does he think about your psychic abilities?"

"At first it was difficult for him to accept. After he personally witnessed things happening that I'd predicted, he became a believer. Now when I suggest he do something or not do it, he never questions me, which is nice."

Marty pulled off onto the gravel road on the outskirts of High Desert and parked in front of the compound. "Home, sweet home," she said. "I'll meet you in the courtyard in a little while, after I call Carl and the book man, and I'll show you photos of what we did today. I also need to send them over to Lucy at the drugstore, so she can develop them, and I can pick them up tomorrow on the way home."

"You're on," Laura said as she opened the gate of the stone fence that surrounded the compound. "Give me twenty minutes."

"Ladies, how was your day?" John asked from the front door of his house. "I heard your car drive up. I hope you worked up an appetite because Max has been helping me, and we're having lamb meatballs in a warm yogurt sauce over egg noodles for dinner. It's a new dish for me, and I need to test it out on you before I put it on The Red Pony's menu. There was some detective here a little while ago who said it smelled so good he'd love an invitation to dinner, so I invited him. I made plenty of it."

Laura and Marty looked at each other in disbelief. "Are you talking about Detective Jeff Combs?" Marty asked.

"Yep. He's the very one. Seemed like a nice enough guy. He was looking for you, Marty. He said something about the Monkey Band. I told him I didn't have a clue what he was talking about. He'll be back about six and asked me to tell you he needed to talk to you."

Swell. Just swell. I hope to heck my eyelid doesn't start twitching, and I can look and act like a normal person, not like some swooning teenager, which is how he makes me feel. I just don't need a distraction like him in my life right now. I haven't even been divorced a year. I remember reading it takes a month for every year you were married to get over someone. Think the article was wrong, because I already am definitely over Scott, and there's no denying that Jeff is very attractive. I also can't deny that there seemed to be some sort of chemistry going on between the two of us when we met this afternoon.

Marty opened the door of her house and turned to wave at Laura and John. "See you in a few minutes. I need to make a couple of phone calls and get into something more comfortable."

CHAPTER THIRTEEN

Marty spent a few minutes petting Duke who had been faithfully watching for her return. When she was gone, his favorite thing to do was to lie down with his chin on his paws and look through the gap under the front fence gate, waiting for her return. From what Laura, Les, and John told her, as soon as he spotted her car, he would jump up and stand next to the gate, his tail wagging furiously in anticipation of her impending arrival. This evening had been no exception.

She put her camera down on the small oak table in the great room, which was another word for a combined living room, dining room, and kitchen, although it wasn't all that great in size. Two small bedrooms and a bathroom completed the house, but it was really all the space she needed. Duke got on his dog bed and looked up at her with his big brown eyes. Whenever Marty spoke to him, his tail thumped as if he could understand every word she was saying. She poured herself a glass of cold chardonnay wine, looked up the name of the antique book expert, called him, and made an appointment with him to appraise the books. The next call she made was to Carl Mitchell, the jewelry expert.

"Palm Springs Antique Shoppe. May I help you?" the voice that answered the phone said.

"Carl Mitchell, please. This is Marty Morgan."

"It's Carl, Marty. What can I do for you this fine evening?"

She told him she was involved in an appraisal and there was, what looked to her, like some very good jewelry in it. "Carl, I took some quick photos of the jewelry. If you have a minute I'd like to send them to you. What's your email address? I'll scan them on my home computer and send them to you right now as an attachment, and hopefully then we can talk about them."

"Sure, there's no one in the shop, so that would be fine." A moment later he said, "Got them. Wow! That's some pretty high end jewelry. I'd swear I've seen a couple of those pieces. What do you need from me?"

"I'm doing an estate appraisal for a man whose mother was murdered. Any chance you could meet me at the house tomorrow morning at eight? I know you like to open your shop at ten, so that should give you plenty of time to do an appraisal of the jewelry pieces. You can send me your appraisal report in the next week or so, and I can attach your report to my appraisal."

"That will work well for me. Why don't you fill me in on the details?"

"A woman by the name of Pam Jensen was murdered, and it's her estate…"

"Wait, you don't need to go any farther. I knew Pam well, and I was shocked and surprised when I read in the local paper she'd been murdered. She frequented my shop and was one of the most astute antique collectors I've ever known. Speaking of her, a kind of funny thing happened to me that she would have appreciated. I had a call earlier today from a man who wanted to know what the pieces from the Meissen Monkey Band were worth. It immediately brought memories of Pam to mind. She told me once that Henry Siegelman wanted to buy three pieces of her Monkey Band set, but she wouldn't sell them to him.

"She invited me to her house once to look at her antiques. I'll never forget the Monkey Band. That set is one of the few things I've ever coveted in all the years I've been in antiques. Whoever inherits her estate will get a real bonus with that. An original set like hers is extremely rare, and hers was in perfect condition."

Marty was quiet for a moment and then she said, "Carl, did you happen to get the name of the person who was inquiring about the Monkey Band set?"

"No, why do you ask?"

"The Monkey Band set is missing from Pam's home. From what I've been able to tell, it's the only thing missing. A friend of hers came to the house today and realized it was gone. I don't know if that's a motive for murder, but it certainly is suspicious. Detective Jeff Combs is coming over to my home in a little while to find out more about the Monkey Band. He's the detective assigned to the case. I'll tell him about the call you received."

"I wish I could help you more, Marty, but I get so many calls from people who want to know how much something is worth that I kind of tune them out unless they want to sell it. I do remember asking the man why he wanted to know, and he said he was just curious. From his response I couldn't tell if he was interested in buying or selling a Monkey Band set, or if he'd seen something about the Monkey Band in an antique magazine and it was nothing more than idle curiosity. Now I wish I'd paid more attention to him, particularly since Pam was murdered."

"Don't beat yourself up about it. You had no way of knowing. Can you tell me anything about a man by the name of Henry Siegelman? Do you know anything about him?"

"I've never met him. He hires people to frequent antique shops and auctions and look for things to add to his collection. It's pretty common knowledge that his love is Meissen, and he's desperate to complete his Monkey Band set. Evidently he's missing three pieces. Other than that, he's kind of a mystery man. Everyone in the antique world knows about him, but nobody seems to actually know him."

"Carl, this just popped into my head because we're dealing with a murder mystery. Do you think he could have been desperate enough to kill in order to complete his set? Maybe not him if he didn't even bother to come to your shop himself, but maybe he could have hired someone?"

"Marty, I can't answer that. Like I said, I've never met the man. I do know collectors often become obsessed with certain antiques, so maybe he was involved in it. I just don't know. I've got to go Marty, a customer just walked in. I know where Pam's home is, and I'll meet you there tomorrow morning at eight. Thanks for thinking of me, and I wish I could have been more helpful to you."

"See you tomorrow, and don't worry, you've been very helpful. Thanks. Enjoy your evening." After she ended the call, she sat for a few moments thinking about what Carl had said.

So Henry Siegelman needs three pieces to complete his collection of the Monkey Band. Wow! I better tell Jeff about that. You never know what someone might do when they become obsessed with something.

CHAPTER FOURTEEN

Okay, Marty thought, *I have to admit I'm looking forward to seeing Jeff again. After all, he's very handsome and maybe, just maybe, there's something going on between the two of us. Laura seems to sense it, and she's usually right. I'm doubly glad he's coming to dinner, because maybe he's heard of Henry Siegelman. Even if he hasn't, I think he'll want to know what Carl told me. Better change clothes and refresh my make-up. If he does want to get to know me, I'll do what I can to look good and give him a reason to. It was pretty apparent that Nikki Bolen was attracted to him.*

She took her hair out of the chignon that she wore it in when she was appraising, so her hair wouldn't get in her eyes. Soft auburn curls framed her face, highlighting her creamy complexion and hazel eyes. Marty put on a jade colored dressy T-shirt that had raglan sleeves and a low vee neck that brought out the green in her eyes. She paired it with white jeans and white sandals. She looked at her image in the mirror and decided for a woman who was going to be fifty in a few months, she didn't look that bad.

Marty opened the front door of her house and walked over to the picnic table where Les, John, Max, and Laura were sitting, a bottle of wine already on the table. "Wow, you look great. All dolled up for the detective I see," John said with a smirk on his face.

"I am not dolled up for anyone. I simply needed to change clothes, and I decided to put on a little make-up. Honest, it's no big deal."

The three of them grinned and exchanged knowing looks. "Okay, Marty, whatever you say. We won't make a big deal of it when lover boy comes for dinner tonight," John said.

Marty pelted him with some peanuts he'd set out on the table. "Let's get one thing straight. He is not my lover boy, and I have no intention of having him become my lover boy, contrary to what that nosy, mouthy sister of mine probably told you."

Laura put her hands up in self-defense. "Marty, I simply mentioned that the detective who was coming to dinner tonight seemed more interested in you than in solving the murder case. Would that be a fair assessment? Oh, and I didn't even mention your twitching eyelid."

"This conversation is officially over," Marty said. She turned to John. "Laura and I had something for lunch today that I think needs to be on The Red Pony's menu." She told him about the Mexican Eggs Benedict Rosa had made for them. "Honestly John, after I took just one bite I could see it on your menu. You could make the cornbread ahead of time, get everything ready, and all you'd have to do when somebody placed an order would be to poach the eggs. I think it would be perfect for you. Anyway, here's the recipe," she said, handing him a piece of paper.

"Boss, sounds danged good. Let's fix it and see fer ourselves," Max said, his weathered face crinkled in a smile.

"You know me. I'm always open for a new dish," John said. "Thanks, Marty."

The small bell that was next to the compound gate rang. "Looks like lover boy, sorry Marty, meant to say that Detective Jeff Combs is here," John said." I'll get it." A moment later they heard him greet Jeff and say, "How thoughtful of you. Yes, this is a perfect wine to go with the lamb. As a matter of fact, if I had to pick one out, it's exactly what I would have chosen. Thank you. We're pretty casual here, so just have a seat at the picnic table in the courtyard. Here's a glass."

"Don't mind if I do, since I'm off duty. Greetings. I've met everyone except you two," he said to Les and Max, extending his hand. "I'm Jeff Combs."

"Nice to meet you. I'm Les, the resident guy who plays with colors on canvas and this is Max, John's sous chef. Welcome to the compound."

Jeff turned and smiled at Marty. "It's nice to see you again, Marty. You look beautiful. If you don't mind I need to pick your brain about some issues involved in the Pam Jensen murder investigation. Have you told the others about the appraisal you were on today?"

"No, as a matter of fact I got tied up on the phone, and I've only been here a couple of minutes."

He turned to the others. "I'm sorry to do this at dinner, but I need some information from Marty about something called the Monkey Band."

"The Monkey Band? I've never heard the term. What is it?" John said.

"I'll get to it in a minute, or Marty can tell you later. Here's a little background. A woman was murdered last week in Palm Springs, and Marty's appraising the items contained in her home. The case was assigned to me, but I've been unable to come up with a motive or a suspect. Looks like that's changed based on what I learned today. I found out this afternoon that the decedent changed her Will just a few days before she was murdered. Since her lawyer filed it with the court this afternoon, it's now a matter of public record. The interesting thing is that her son and daughter will get only half of what they would have gotten if she hadn't changed it."

"Do you think that makes her son, Jim, a suspect?" Marty asked.

"Yes. I did a little research on him after I found out about it. Apparently he's had a number of failed business ventures and has been divorced twice. I asked around about him, and the Palm Springs business community is not all that enamored of him. One person I talked to had been a good friend of his stepfather, Brian Jensen, and this person told me Brian said he would never lend Jim another cent, and he had instructed his wife to do the same."

"So, if he were to lose half of his inheritance, that might be grounds for murder. Would I be right?" John asked.

"Possibly. You know the law. Everyone is innocent until proven guilty, but he is someone I intend to spend a little time with tomorrow."

"You might also want to spend a little time with the housekeeper, Rosa." Laura said.

"Why?"

She sighed. "Jeff, have you had any experience with the psychic world?"

"Absolutely none. Are you talking about crystal balls and tarot cards and stuff like that?"

"Well, it's complicated," Laura said. "There are so many different things that can fall into the overall psychic category, some of which are legitimate and others aren't." She told him about how she had been tested at UCLA, and that sometimes she knew things or felt them before those things actually occurred.

"From what I'm hearing, I'm guessing you feel something isn't quite right with the housekeeper, would I be right?" Jeff asked.

"This conversation is driving me nuts, "John said. "I feel like I'm watching a movie about a murder mystery, but if we want to eat before it's bed time, Max and I better leave and get dinner ready. We'll be back in about half an hour, and Marty, thanks for the recipe.

I'll put it on the menu and try it out. Might even call it Marty's Mexican Eggs Benedict."

"Don't think that would make Rosa very happy, but thanks for the thought."

Laura continued, "Here's what I've experienced about this murder case and the appraisal which seems to be somehow connected to the murder. Last night I had a vision, a dream, or some kind of a feeling, whatever you want to call it, that Marty would be involved with things that were related to the murder. However, in the dream, Marty wouldn't be able to appraise the most important thing to be appraised, because it was gone. When that woman Nikki was at the house this afternoon and told us the Monkey Band set was missing, I started to wonder if that's what the murder is about and the reason Marty couldn't appraise the most important thing because it had been stolen."

"My brain tends to think in logical ways rather than psychic ways, and that seems like a pretty logical assumption. What about Rosa?" Jeff asked.

"When I first met her I told Marty I felt guilt coming off of her. You probably don't think much of people seeing auras…"

Jeff interrupted her. "I have no clue what an aura even is."

"It's a halo-like color that usually surrounds the person. When I look at a person and see an aura, it tells me all kinds of things about them. Rosa's was black. That's not a color you want to have, in fact it's the worst color a person can have. It can signify anger, depression, hatred, or anything that's really bad. The feeling I got from Rosa's aura was one of guilt. I don't think she had anything to do with the murder, but she definitely feels guilty about something. If the Monkey Band was stolen, and it appears to have been, I think Rosa knows something about it. When Nikki told us it was gone, I happened to be looking at Rosa. Her hand went involuntarily to her heart and she turned pale. In psychic speak, it would be called a tell. In other words she had an involuntary reaction to what was being said."

"Well, that's interesting. So now I guess I should be looking at both Pam's son, Jim, as well as her housekeeper."

"Yes, and I have to tell you I mentioned to Marty when we were in the driveway and Jim drove in behind us, that I didn't have a good feeling about him. My psychic sense tells me there is something more about Jim that may be of interest to you other than his dissatisfaction with his mother having changed her Will."

"Let me add to your list of possible suspects as I think there might be one or two others for you to be looking at as well," Marty said and told him about her earlier conversation with Carl. "It's too bad he didn't get the name of the person who called him and inquired about the value of Monkey Band pieces, but I think you can probably find out some information about the man named Henry Siegelman."

"That name rings a bell, but I can't place it. Marty, do you have a computer?"

"Yes, why?"

"Well, from what John said we have a little time before dinner. Would you mind if I Googled him? I'd be interested in knowing just how much information there is on him."

Marty stood up. "My computer's in my office." She turned to Laura, "Call us when John's ready. The one thing I don't want to do is make the chef angry by being late to dinner!" she said laughing as Jeff followed her into her home.

CHAPTER FIFTEEN

"I like the way you've decorated your home, Marty. It's very much in keeping with the desert," Jeff said as he looked at the Navajo rugs on the tile floor and the soft off-white furniture. "Those pillows look great on the couch. Since you're the authority on antiques, are they antique, too?"

"Yes. They're made from Kilim rugs which usually come from Turkey. A lot of people think the designs of the Navajo rugs that are so collectible were based on the Kilim rugs. I found several that were inexpensive because they were in such bad shape, so I took the good parts and had them made into pillows. I like how they play against the Navajo rugs. Here's my computer and it's already on, so feel free to search for whatever you need. Where do you start when you're doing something like this?"

"I'll begin by simply putting his name in the search box and see what comes up." Jeff sat down at the desk where the computer was located and entered Henry Siegelman's name. He clicked on several sites, and after a few minutes he turned to where Marty was quietly sitting and watching.

"This is interesting. He lives not too far from here, in La Quinta. That's where I started my police career before I moved to Palm Springs. Evidently his parents were very wealthy, and he inherited a great deal of money when they died at an early age, while he was still in college. According to what I'm seeing, he's never worked. It says he's a big player in the stock market, but the thing that has the most bearing on this case is every article states that his antique and art collection is one of the finest in the world. He's recognized as being one of the foremost experts on Meissen china and apparently has one of the best private collections of it."

"Do any of the articles mention the Monkey Band?"

"No. I think I'll look into this more when I get home. I know I've heard his name before, and I can't quite place where or when I heard it. Whatever it was I heard, I guess it's floating around out there somewhere in the ether. Maybe I can't remember because you're having a distracting effect on me."

"I'm what?" Marty asked, wide-eyed. "I'm not doing anything but sitting here."

"That's enough to distract me. I'm quickly finding out I'm not at my best when I'm around you. I feel like some gawky teenage boy, doing and saying everything wrong. Marty, I really would like to see you and show you I'm not just some guy on the make. I don't know what it is about you, but I feel like I've known you forever. I've never felt quite so comfortable with a woman."

"Well, thank you for the compliment, but we don't know anything about each other."

"I know, and that's the beauty of it. We can tell each other our life stories, and neither one of us will have heard it before. I suppose that's the advantage of not being with someone for a long time. I always wondered what old married couples talked about because they'd each probably heard the other one's story a million times. Actually, I think it would be nice to hear your story a couple of times."

"Jeff, this is a little fast. We haven't even known each other for eight hours."

"That might be true, but at our age I can't see any reason to play some game. My parents got married after they'd only known each other for six weeks, and they were married for over fifty years. No one gave their marriage a week. Mom and dad outlasted all the critics and gossips.

"I'd be lying if I told you I didn't want to see you again," Marty said, "but let's take it slow and easy. We've got plenty of time."

"Easy for you to say. You probably have a bunch of guys standing in line, and I'm at the back of the line."

"Don't think so." She laughed and added, "As a matter of fact, I'm somewhat newly divorced and a real newbie at middle age relationships. I haven't a clue where to go with this."

He stood up from the chair in front of the desk and walked over to her. "Well, for starters, how about this?" he said as he pulled her up and lightly kissed her.

Oh lord, I didn't expect this. If we don't go out to the courtyard right now, I might just give them a reason to call him Lover Boy.

She pulled away. "I think we better go outside. Dinner's probably ready, and I know from experience that while John is the most giving person in the world and one of the best chefs I know, he definitely is not happy if someone is late to dinner, but I think I'd like a rain check on the follow-up to that kiss," she said smiling up at him.

"Lady, it would be my pleasure," he said, opening the door for her.

CHAPTER SIXTEEN

"John, I don't consider myself to be a food connoisseur, but this meatball dish is fantastic. What's in it?" Jeff asked.

"That's exactly what a chef wants to hear. Thank you! It's a Mideastern dish consisting of lamb meatballs in a warm yogurt dill sauce. The recipe had an option to serve it over rice or noodles. I opted for egg noodles and think it works. If the five of you like it, I'll add it to the truck's menu."

"Don't have to ask me twice, Boss. This sucker's a real hit. Got a lotta Mideasterners for customers who'll be all over this like flies on..."

"That's enough, Max. We're in the company of ladies," John interrupted, grinning at his redneck cook.

"Sorry, Boss," Max said abashedly.

"I believe I can speak for all of us, John, when I tell you this is definitely a hit! I often make meatballs ahead of time, so it should work on the truck. Actually, I imagine you could make most of it ahead of time and even freeze the meatballs in your freezer at home here," Laura said.

"I think you're absolutely right. I see no reason why I couldn't even cook the meatballs and freeze them. That way, all I'd have to do is warm them. The sauce will keep for several days. I don't want to freeze the yogurt, but I could make batches of noodles and keep them warm. My loyal customers will have this treat beginning day after tomorrow. All I need to do is buy the ingredients."

"Jeff," Les asked, "did you find anything on the computer about that Henry guy?"

"Nothing more than what we'd heard. He's a wealthy collector who lives in La Quinta. That's about it. I need to talk to him, and I want to talk to the housekeeper, Rosa, as well. Something is nipping at my heels about this Henry guy, but I can't come up with it. I'm going to do a little research tonight when I get home, speaking of which, it's time for me to be going. I can't thank you all enough for your hospitality. I've really enjoyed this evening, and this courtyard is magical," he said looking around at the twinkling lights and lanterns. "I could stay here forever and be happy."

Laura, Les, and John looked at each other and smiled knowing it wasn't the twinkling lights at the compound that interested Jeff. "You're always welcome here. Please feel free to come back anytime," Laura said.

"With an invitation like that, how could I refuse? Of course I need to check with Marty. Marty, would it be okay with you if I come back?" the handsome middle-aged detective asked. Laura was watching him closely and noticed how he rubbed his thumb and right index finger together. It was a tell. She knew from experience his particular tell indicated he was nervous.

So Mr. Suave Detective is not quite as sure of himself as he appears. I like that about him, Laura thought.

Marty smiled warmly and answered, "Yes, and I'll be interested to hear what you find out about Henry. I've never been involved in a murder case before, and I'm finding it fascinating."

"It may be fascinating to you, but for me it's pretty frustrating.

While we're enjoying a wonderful dinner, there's a killer on the loose. That thought never comforts me when I'm working a case." He stood up. "Again, thanks to all of you for making me feel so welcome. Marty, want to walk me to the gate?"

She stood up and so did Duke. As they were walking to the gate, Duke managed to get between them. "What's up with him? Is he some kind of a guard dog?" Jeff asked, grinning at her.

"Not to my knowledge. Seems like Labs are pretty friendly, and I've never heard of any of them being on a police force. I've never seen him like this." Duke looked up at Jeff and growled.

"Well, from the sound of him, I think he'd make a pretty good police dog. I'd like to kiss you goodnight, but I'm not so sure that's a good idea at the moment. Does he do this with all your male friends?"

"Considering that you're the first male friend I've had since I bought him, I don't have any history on his behavior in that context."

"I'm going to be coming back, so he better get used to me. Next time I'll bring some dog treats and see if I can worm my way into his good graces that way."

"Detective, I think there's another name for that kind behavior. Rather imagine in your line of work it would be called blackmail or some such thing and would probably be illegal."

"Marty, I would prefer to call it a bribe. That word doesn't quite have the negative connotation that blackmail does, and really it is more of a bribe than blackmail."

"Well, it might not be good for your reputation if it gets out you're using bribes to gain favor with a nice, friendly black Lab. I'd be careful who you say that to. I'll pretend like I didn't hear it. Could cause some problems in your line of work," she said laughing. "If you find something out about Siegelman, I'd like to know."

"If you don't hear from me tonight I'll see you tomorrow. I definitely want to talk to Rosa. See you then." He opened the gate and walked out to his car. Duke never took his eyes off of him until he'd gotten in his car, and then he sat down, raised his head to Marty and silently asked for an ear scratch.

"Duke, it's all right. I think he's a good man, and I think we'll be seeing more of him. You're going to have to get used to him," she said as they walked into her house.

CHAPTER SEVENTEEN

Marty had just turned the lamp off on her nightstand when her cell phone rang. She reached over and answered it.

"This is Marty."

"Hi, it's Jeff. I'm sorry to call this late, but I told you I'd let you know if I found out something about Henry Siegelman. I did."

"Actually, I've been doing some research on the appraisal, and I just turned off my light, so it's not a problem. What did you find out?"

"I told you something was bothering me about the name Henry Siegelman, and it came to me on the way home. I remembered a theft case one of my friends in the department worked on years ago when I first started out and was with the La Quinta Police Department. I'm sure you know it's a pretty wealthy area, and some very valuable California Impressionist paintings had been stolen from a gallery. I won't bother you with the details, but the department was able to catch the person who committed the theft and arrest him."

"I'm sorry, Jeff, I must be missing something. I don't see a tie-in to Henry Siegelman from what you're telling me."

"Stay with me. A few months later I had to go to court in La

Quinta for my divorce, which is another story. We'll go into that another time. Anyway, my friend and I were having a couple of beers after I'd been to court, and he told me more about the case. The guy they'd arrested for the art heist sang like a canary about who'd hired him. He told my friend, the lead detective, he'd been hired by a guy who worked for a man named Henry Siegelman. My friend told me they'd tried to get something on Siegelman, so they could make a case against him, but he had a very good attorney, and there never was enough evidence to charge him, although they were able to make a case against both the art thief and the guy who hired him at Siegelman's request."

"Wow! That could mean Henry Siegelman's possibly behind the Monkey Band theft. Maybe he hired someone to steal it and the thief encountered Mrs. Jensen in the process and killed her. You're the expert here. Would that be a fair assessment of what might have happened?"

"Yes, you're right and you're thinking like a detective. It very well could have happened that way. When I talk to Rosa tomorrow I want to find out if Mrs. Jensen usually went out at night. Maybe the thief was banking on her being gone. No one has said anything about her having a male friend, but maybe that's a possibility, and if it is, and the thief knew about her male friend, he might have been planning on her being out for the evening with her friend."

"What about the guy who went to prison for the art theft? The one your friend arrested? Could you talk to him?"

"I wish I could, but I called my friend tonight, and he told me after the guy got out of prison he was murdered last year in a drug deal gone bad. I'm going to talk to Henry Siegelman tomorrow, but if he was able to hide his involvement in that case, there's nothing that leads me to believe he won't be able to do it again. Unless I can find something solid on him, there's no way the District Attorney will charge him in this case. There's simply not enough to go on."

"So if you can't find out something, and if Henry Siegelman did it, he not only will go free, he'll also have the Monkey Band set. Is that right?"

"Fraid so. Believe me, I don't like this any more than you do, but if I can't find the person who actually stole the set and murdered Mrs. Jensen, there is no way I can make a case against Henry Siegelman."

"Well, that sounds pretty lousy."

"Trust me, it is. That's the down side of this business. It's pretty exhilarating when you solve a case and the bad guy does time, but when you suspect someone had a hand in a crime and you can't find enough evidence to charge them, it's pretty frustrating."

"I'll keep my eyes and ears open tomorrow. Laura's going with me on the appraisal again. Maybe her psychic abilities will kick in, and she can come up with something. Sounds like you could use some sixth sense help on this case."

He laughed. "For my own sake, I wish I believed in that stuff a little more. Maybe that's what I need to solve the case. See you tomorrow. Sleep well."

"Good night, Jeff." *And maybe that's exactly what you do need to solve this case,* she thought, setting her phone on the nightstand as she turned off the light. Tomorrow promised to be another exciting day.

CHAPTER EIGHTEEN

"Ready, Laura?" Marty asked, as she lightly knocked on her sister's door. "I told Carl I'd meet him at 8:00 at the Jensen home, and I don't want to be late."

"Yes, I wanted to look a couple of things up before we went out there this morning, but I'm ready now. I know you'll think it's stupid, but there's such a thing as a protection chant. I couldn't quite remember it, so I looked it up and jotted it down. Given everything that's happened at that house, I thought we could use it," she said as they walked out to Marty's car.

"Well, thanks, I guess. I don't know a thing about chants and protection. I'll leave it up to you. I did talk to Jeff last night and found out a little more information about Henry Siegelman." On the drive to the Jensen home she filled Laura in on what Jeff had told her.

"What I'm hearing from you is that this thing may never be solved. Is that what you got from talking to him?"

"Yes and no. If Henry Siegelman is behind it, there's a good chance it won't be solved if it's anything like the case Jeff told me about that involved him. Then again, it could be someone else. I had the feeling that Jeff almost hopes it is. Oh good, Carl's already here. I don't think you've met him before."

"How did you find him?"

"There's an antique appraiser society in town, and I joined it. We have a monthly dinner meeting. It really is a good way to network and find people you'd like to work with. For some reason Carl and I hit it off. He owns the Palm Springs Antique Shoppe, a really high end antique shop, but his love is jewelry. He's certified by two societies in that area, but he's also knowledgeable about a lot of other things. I've helped him with a couple of appraisals, and he's helped me. We work well together. You may not have much to do while we're appraising the jewelry, because I'll be photographing it for him to save him some time."

"I thought you took pictures of it yesterday and sent it to him."

"Those weren't good enough for an appraisal. I just wanted him to get a sense of what was in the jewelry collection."

They got out of the car and walked up to the gate where an older nondescript looking man with thinning red hair and a large belly was standing, wearing a black and white polka dot bow tie and a bright red vest under a white seersucker suit. "Carl, I want you to meet my sister, Laura. She's acting as my assistant, Laura, Carl Mitchell."

"Happy to meet you Carl, and I'm also glad to know of a good jewelry appraiser. I work for Alliance Property and Casualty Company. My boss is in charge of deciding which of our clients need appraisals. The turnover for appraisers is pretty high. Seems like a lot of people come to the desert in the late fall or early spring and become enchanted by the weather and decide to move here. The enchantment often fades after they spend a summer here and suffer through days and days of temperatures of over one hundred degrees. A lot of them decide to go back where they came from. I think that's one of the reasons we see such a high turnover of people involved in the appraisal business."

"Nice to meet you, Laura," Carl said. "Here's my business card. Please call me if I can help you." He turned to Marty. "Let's get started. I really don't want to open the shop up late." The gate was open, and they entered the courtyard.

"I called Rosa last night and told her we'd be here early this morning. She must have opened the gate." The front door to the house was open, and they were greeted by Rosa who was standing next to the door.

"Rosa, this is Carl Mitchell. He's going to appraise Mrs. Jensen's jewelry, and I'll be helping him. By the way Carl, her son mentioned she had a ten carat marquise cut diamond ring with a platinum setting that wasn't in the floor safe. He asked me to be on the lookout for it. He opened the safe to show me what was in it, and that's when I decided I needed your expertise. I closed it, and Jim gave me the combination. Let's go back to her bedroom where the safe is. I'll open it, and we can get started."

"Ms. Morgan," Rosa said. "I remember seeing Mrs. Jensen wearing that ring. It was one of her favorites, but I haven't seen it since she died. I thought you might like something to eat this morning, so I made some sweet rolls and a pot of coffee. May I bring you some?"

"That would be wonderful. Thanks!" They walked down the hall to the bedroom, and Marty walked over to where the floor safe was. She took the combination from her purse and opened it. "How do you want to do this, Carl?"

"I'd like you to take one piece of jewelry at a time out of the safe. Place each piece on this black velvet cloth I brought and photograph it. We'll follow that process until you've photographed each piece, and I've examined each one. I want frontal and side photos as well as any shots of identifying marks. Make sense?"

"Yes, here's the first piece. Let me photograph it, and we'll go from there."

Carl had just finished with the last piece when Laura walked into the bedroom holding a butcher's knife and a cutting board in her hands. "Good grief, Laura, what are you doing?" Marty asked, at a loss as to why her mild-mannered sister was walking into the room with a butcher's knife in her hand.

"You haven't found the missing ring, have you?" Laura asked.

Carl and Marty both shook their heads, indicating no.

"I know where it is. I just had a vision that told me where to look for it."

"What are you talking about?" Carl asked. "I've seen some pretty strange things while I've been in this business, but I've never had anyone walk into a room where I was conducting an appraisal with a butcher's knife and a cutting board."

"Carl, we don't tell many people this, but in addition to working for an insurance company, Laura's a psychic, and that's what she means by a vision," Marty said.

"Marty, this is way over my head, and I'm not sure I'm comfortable with it. Laura, are you sure you know what you're doing?" Carl asked.

"Yes. Do you see that styrofoam wig stand at the end of the closet shelf? It's shaped in the form of a human head so a wig can be displayed on it. Carl, you're taller than we are, would you please lift it down and put it on the cutting board?"

Carl stood for a moment clearly trying to decide whether or not Laura was deranged. "Carl, please," Marty said. "I've learned if Laura says she wants someone to do something strange, there's a very good reason for it."

He stared at her for a moment then lifted the styrofoam head off the shelf and asked, "Do you want me to put it on the board upright or lay it down?"

"Roll it over so the back of the head is upright, and I'd like both of you to take a couple of steps back." They did as she asked, and a moment later she raised the knife over her head and brought it down, splitting the wig stand from top to bottom. A ring with a large diamond in it rolled out of the split head. "Here's the missing diamond ring. Do you want me to put it on the black velvet so it can be photographed?" Laura asked.

"How did you know that's where it was? I've never seen anything like this in all my life. My mind is having a hard time accepting what my eyes just saw," Carl blurted out with an amazed look on his face.

"Thanks, Laura. We'll take it from here. Knew there was a reason I wanted you on this appraisal. It's not uncommon for women who live alone to hide something valuable in unusual places like the pocket of their bathrobe or some other place, although I've never seen anything quite like this." She photographed the ring and handed it to Carl whose eyes were uncommonly large as he stared, gape-mouthed, at the large sparkling diamond ring.

"I'm almost afraid to touch it. Laura, could this thing be hexed or something? I guess what I'm asking is if I'm going to have something horrible happen to me because I'm about to touch it?"

"No, I did a protection chant before I came into the room. We're all going to be just fine."

"You did a protection chant," Carl said. "Swell. I can't even believe I heard those words, much less that I'm saying them. I've heard of a sixth sense, but this is definitely the first time I've ever experienced it. Do you realize if you hadn't found that ring it probably would have been thrown out when the room's unneeded items like the wig stand were cleaned out and dumped in the trash? Wow! I'm impressed."

Carl finished up his examination of the ring and said, "I need to leave. Marty, it should take me about a week to get my report to you. Thanks again for asking me to do this. Laura, I should say it's been a pleasure to meet you, but instead I think I'll say you've provided me with the most extraordinary experience I've ever had in my life, and I rather doubt anyone would believe me even if I tried to tell them about it. I know you two ladies have a lot more to do here, so I'll let myself out."

"Thanks, Carl. I'll be talking to you," Marty said.

He walked out of the room, shaking his head and mumbling to himself.

CHAPTER NINETEEN

"Laura, I don't know if Carl will ever accept another appraisal of mine after you broke open the styrofoam head with the butcher's knife and found the ring."

"Yeah, it was kind of exciting," Laura said, laughing, "Now what?"

"As long as we're in the bedroom, I'd like to do the furniture and decorative items and finish up with the antique perfume bottle collection on the vanity." The master bathroom was a huge room with a tiled floor, a large tiled shower with six jet sprays, a claw foot tub, and an antique vanity which displayed the perfume bottles. The bathroom overlooked the hills and the only window coverings were white silk tieback drapes. Brightly colored blooming orchids were placed throughout the room.

"Sounds good. Shall I be the official holder of the tape measure like yesterday?"

"That would work for me. We'll start with the bed." For the next two hours Laura held the tape measure and whatever else Marty asked of her while Marty painstakingly took the dimensions of the item and anything pertinent to it, recorded it, and photographed it.

At noon, Rosa walked into the bedroom and said, "I'd like to fix lunch for you, if that's all right. It will be ready in about twenty minutes."

"That would be great, and those sweet rolls were wonderful. Thank you. Actually your timing's perfect. I'll finish up everything but the perfume bottle collection before lunch, and after lunch we can tackle it."

Twenty minutes later, they walked into the breakfast nook where Rosa had set out lunch for them on the table. "This looks fabulous Rosa. Thank you so much," Marty said, "What do we have here?"

"I made stuffed avocados with a chicken salad filling and a fruit compote. The drink is a virgin pomegranate blueberry rickey. Mrs. Jensen had one almost every day at lunch. I hope you like it."

"Thank you, I'm sure we will."

A few minutes later the buzzer rang, indicating there was someone at the gate. "Who's there?" Rosa asked as she pressed the intercom.

"It's Detective Combs."

"I'll open the gate for you and meet you at the front door."

A few minutes later Jeff walked into the breakfast nook. He greeted Marty and Laura and turned to Rosa. "If you have any more avocados and fruit, I would love some. I haven't had time for lunch, and it looks like it's going to be a busy afternoon."

"I have plenty. I'll be right back." Jeff sat down at the table, "Well ladies, how was your morning?"

"Pretty unbelievable. You should have been here," Marty said. She told him about the diamond ring, how Laura had a vision of where it was hidden, and Carl's reaction to it.

"I'm with Carl, but I have to admire him for staying in the room. No offense, Laura, but if you'd walked into a room where I was with a butcher's knife, I'm not sure I would have stayed around to see what was in the wig stand. That's pretty unbelievable. I'm kind of sorry I missed it. Would have made a great water cooler story."

Rosa set a place for him and put a luncheon plate in front of him along with a big glass of the rickey. He took a huge sip. "Rosa, that's not only delicious, but it's one of the most refreshing things I've ever had."

"I agree, Rosa. If you have time, I know someone who would love to have that recipe," Marty said. She turned to Laura and Jeff. "Here's another one I can see being served at The Red Pony."

"Certainly, Ms. Morgan. Mrs. Jensen has a copy machine in her office. I'll make a photocopy for you."

"Thanks. Jeff, how was your morning?" Marty asked.

He put one of his hands out in front of him, palm facing down, and wiggled it back and forth as if to say, so-so. "I called Henry Siegelman early this morning and told him I wanted to meet with him this morning. The nice thing about being a detective is that a person will generally agree to see you. The not so nice thing about being a detective is that the smart ones have their attorney there and don't answer many questions on the attorney's advice. Henry is one of the smart ones."

"I'm picking up that his attorney was there when you arrived. Would I be right?" Laura asked.

"You don't need to be a psychic to figure that out. Yes. Of course Henry denied any involvement in Mrs. Jensen's death. He said he'd approached her several times about buying the three pieces of the Meissen Monkey Band that his collection lacked. He said she'd told him she had no intention of ever selling them. I asked him if I could see his set. He showed it to me, and I have to say, I don't know a thing about antiques, but the Monkey Band is kind of cute. These little monkeys, and I mean little, they're only about five inches high or so, are charming in their little 18th century outfits and playing their various different musical instruments. I can see where he'd want to complete the set."

"So what do you do now?" Marty asked.

"There's not much I can do unless something breaks. I have an appointment with Pam's son, Jim Warren, this afternoon. I'd like to know where he was the night of the murder. I'm also curious how he's taking the news that his mother signed a Will which nullified the one he has, and he stands to inherit half of what he thought he was going to get."

"I'm glad you're the one who will be talking to him and not me. He'd probably be number one on my list of suspects," Laura said.

"Coming from anyone but you, I'd take that lightly. With what I've seen and I'm hearing about you, I kind of wish you hadn't said that," Jeff chuckled. "Since you feel that way, I'll be very careful when I interview him, although people tend to put on their best face when the detective comes calling." Rosa walked over to the table and put a plate of cookies on it. "Rosa, if you have a couple of minutes, I'd like to talk to you. You may know something that's more important than you think."

"Certainly, Detective Combs. May I clear the dishes first?"

"Of course. While you're doing that, we can enjoy these cookies. They look delicious. I never met Mrs. Jensen, but from the pictures I've seen of her she didn't look the least bit overweight, but after eating this lunch, I don't know how she managed to stay so slim and trim."

Rosa laughed and carried a load of dishes over to the sink.

"Well, ladies, enjoy the rest of your appraising. I'm going to talk to Rosa, and then it will probably be time for my meeting with Jim. I'll call you later. Marty, I'd like to know how the rest of the appraisal goes today."

"Actually, why don't you join us for dinner tonight?" Laura said. "John mentioned he was making a special dish tonight, and I've never had one of his special dishes that wasn't fabulous. Plus, he always makes more than enough."

"You're definitely a psychic. I was angling for an invitation, but I just wasn't sure how to go about it."

"Consider it done. Marty, let's go. I'm interested in the antique perfume bottle collection. Meet you in the master bathroom." She stood up from the table and walked away.

I hope it's okay with you that I wangled an invitation to dinner," Jeff said.

"Absolutely. I was trying to think of a way to do it without risking the three of them making a big deal about it. You saved me the embarrassment. Thanks, and I look forward to seeing you this evening."

"That makes two of us," he said, lightly brushing her cheek with the back of his hand and then walking into the living room where Rosa was waiting for him.

CHAPTER TWENTY

"Rosa, this shouldn't take long, but I'd be remiss if I didn't interview you, because you, more than anyone else, know the details of Mrs. Jensen's activities prior to her death. First of all, how long have you been working for Mrs. Jensen?" Jeff asked.

"I started working for Mr. and Mrs. Jensen ten years ago," she answered in a soft voice, avoiding his eyes.

"How many days a week did you work for them, what hours did you work for them, and are they the only ones you work for?"

"I'm here five days a week, from eight in the morning until five in the evening. They always gave me the weekends off. You see, I have two little granddaughters that my husband and I are raising. I don't work for anyone else."

"Tell me what you did for the Jensens."

"I made certain the house was always clean and that the collections were always dusted. I usually made lunch for Mrs. Jensen if she didn't have other plans."

"So as part of your duties, you regularly dusted the different collections, is that correct?"

"Yes, as I told you yesterday I usually dusted the collections once every week or so. I probably dusted the perfume bottle collection weekly because it wasn't under glass. The Meissen collection was behind glass and didn't get as dusty."

"Tell me about the Meissen collection."

"Mrs. Jensen loved to collect things, but the Meissen collection was her favorite. She was always getting calls from antique dealers or auction houses telling her about different Meissen pieces they had available. She occasionally bought from them. She subscribed to a number of antique magazines and was on the mailing list for catalogues from all the major auction houses. She often told me how lucky she was that her husband was so wealthy and never put any restrictions on what she bought. She told me it made him happy to see her enjoy something so much."

"When you left the house on the evening Mrs. Jensen was murdered, did you observe anything strange?"

Jeff noticed that one of her hands was on top of the other one, clutching it so tightly her knuckles were white. The sheen of perspiration on her upper lip had intensified. She answered, "No, sir, when I left she was here. She said she wouldn't be going out that night and told me she'd see me in the morning. When I came back the next morning she was in her bedroom, dead."

"What did you do when you found her?"

"I called 911 and pretty soon a lot of policemen and other people were here."

"Let me change the subject for a moment. I noticed a security alarm when I came in today. I assume you knew the code and how to arm it and disarm it. Would that be correct?"

"Yes, that's correct."

"When you left in the evenings, did you arm it?"

"I usually did, although for the past couple of months Mr. Jensen's ex-partner, George Ellis, usually took her to dinner. I always asked her if she wanted me to arm it or if she would take care of it."

"And the night she was murdered?"

"She asked me to arm it, because she was staying in for the evening and would not be going out to dinner with George Ellis."

"And do you know why she wasn't going out to dinner with George Ellis when she'd been doing so for some time?"

"I'm not sure, but I overheard her talking to her friend, Nikki Bolen. She's the one who was here yesterday."

"Yes, I know Nikki Bolen."

"Well, she told Mrs. Bolen that George wanted to marry her, and she had turned him down. She said she had no idea he felt that way about her."

Jeff continued to carefully watch Rosa. He could tell she was nervous about something, but he didn't know what. She began to blink rapidly.

"Rosa, I've been in this business long enough to know when someone is withholding information from me, and I know you are. Why don't you tell me what you know? I promise whatever it is, no one will know what you've told me."

She began to sob softly and said in a whisper. "I can't say anything. He said he was going to hurt me or my granddaughters. I promised I wouldn't say anything, but I'm responsible for Mrs. Jensen's death. I intentionally didn't turn on the alarm like she asked me to."

"Rosa, I can get round-the-clock protection for you and your granddaughters, but I need to know what you know. If I don't have that information, I can't help you. Remember, whoever it was who said that has to know you're talking to the police, and it's been my experience that they don't keep their promises. There's a very good chance he's afraid you'll talk to the police, and he'll kill you anyway. I don't know your marital situation, but that might make it very difficult for your granddaughters. Please, tell me what you know, and I'll help you," he said in a friendly, coaxing voice.

Tears slowly ran down her cheeks. "I've never done anything like this in my life. My granddaughter needs surgery, and we don't have the money. My husband, Julio, has been out of work for months, and we can barely make it through the week. We've been living on what Mrs. Jensen paid me." She stopped and pulled a Kleenex out of her pocket, wiping her eyes.

"Would you like me to get you a glass of water?" Jeff asked.

"No, I'll be fine. I'm just so scared."

"That's perfectly normal. Now tell me what happened."

Rosa took a deep breath and then told him about a man named Lou who had approached her and given her $5,000 and how she'd taken $45,000 from him the following afternoon after she agreed to his request to not turn on the alarm. "He must have thought Mrs. Jensen would be out to dinner like she was most nights, and he killed her when she found him stealing the Monkey Band. I know that's what happened. I might just as well have killed her myself. It's all my fault."

"You did something wrong, Rosa, but you didn't kill her. You said his name was Lou and that you called him. I'd like his telephone number although I'm sure he changes phones every couple of days, and I'd be willing to bet that's not his real name. Did he tell you who he was working for?"

"No."

"Have you ever heard of a man named Henry Siegelman?"

"Yes. He's called here several times, and one day when Mrs. Jensen got off the phone she told me she wished he'd never call again. She said all he cared about was completing his Monkey Band set." Suddenly her eyes went wide as she realized the implication of what she'd just said. Her hand went to her throat and she asked with a stunned look on her face, "Do you think this Lou guy was working for Henry Siegelman, and he killed Mrs. Jensen and stole the Monkey Band?"

"I don't know. I wish I could find the man who told you his name was Lou. Since we talked yesterday, have you noticed that anything other than the Monkey Band is gone from any of the rooms?"

"No. That's the only thing I've noticed. Don't you think it's strange in a house filled with antiques that only one thing would be missing? It looks like she was killed for the Monkey Band set since nothing else is gone. I don't know how I can ever live with myself. And my grandbabies? What will happen to them if Lou comes after me and kills me?"

"Rosa, you are not going to be killed. Until this case is solved, I'll provide round-the-clock protection for you and your family. I'll call right now and have a policeman here when you leave. There usually are three shifts, and I'll make sure that while you're here at the house for the next few days, someone else will be guarding your grandchildren. My job is to find out who Lou is and who killed Mrs. Jensen. I understand why you did it. Life isn't always fair, and you did what you had to do for your granddaughter. Desperate times often require some sort of desperate action. Even though I'm a man of the law, if I'd been in your shoes, I just might have done the same thing. As soon as the policeman I mentioned gets here, he'll escort you home, and try not to worry."

Jeff continued, "Rosa, I do need to tell you that if it turns out this Lou guy is the murderer, you would be an accomplice to grand theft." He held up his hands. "Please don't cry. I understand why you did what you did. If you would be willing to testify against Lou if and when he's identified and caught, I won't arrest you. I'll need your testimony at the trial. I know it's a little soon to talk about this, but keep it in the back of your mind."

"Thank you, detective. You've been very kind," she said, tears slowly rolling down her cheeks. She walked into the kitchen, looking like an old woman, beaten by the world.

CHAPTER TWENTY-ONE

"As you well know, I'm not an antique collector, but these bottles are charming. Tell me something about them," Laura said, "and while you're at it, what do you want me to do here?"

"First of all, I'd like you to put each bottle on either this white piece of cotton fabric or on this black velvet piece. Spread it out, so I can photograph the bottle. If it's a clear bottle or a white bottle, put it on the black velvet. Like Carl, I always carry a piece of white fabric and some black velvet with me for use as a backdrop when I'm photographing small items.

"This is probably the finest perfume bottle collection I've ever seen. I remember going out on an appraisal years ago and the client had an extensive perfume bottle collection. The woman was paranoid about it. She told me she lived for that collection, and every spare minute she had she spent studying auction catalogues and going online to see if any new bottles had come on the market, but the reason I remember that particular appraisal so well is that she told me I couldn't touch any of the bottles. She said she would stay in the room with me the whole time while I appraised the collection to make sure I didn't lay one finger on any of the bottles."

"Don't you have to look for identifying marks, and aren't they often found on the bottom of the bottles?"

"Exactly. If something had ever happened to any of those bottles, I'm not sure the insurance company would have paid a cent based on all the caveats I put in the appraisal report about not being able to see the identifying marks, etc. I've often wondered whatever happened to her. I hope she and her collection are happy, because I think that's about all she had.

"Anyway, you asked about antique perfume bottles. They were made in all kinds of mediums, including glass, silver, metal, art glass, cut glass, pressed glass, porcelain, and enamel. Even Meissen made perfume bottles and unless I'm way off, I'd be willing to bet that figurine towards the back of the collection depicting a monk carrying a young girl on his back is a Meissen. Yes," she said, picking it up and looking at the bottom, "there are the crossed swords in the underglaze blue, the early mark. Believe me, a Meissen perfume bottle made in the 18th century is hugely desirable. I wonder if Henry Siegelman knows about it. If he does, I'm sure he'd want to add it to his collection."

"I'd love to see his collection," Laura said, "but even the thought of him fills my mind with the color black. I don't need to be around that kind of dark energy."

"If he had something to do with the theft and the murder, I would think black would be the operative color for him. Okay, let's get started. I just did a quick count, and we're looking at over two hundred pieces. That's going to take at least three hours. We can probably do the perfume bottle collection and then finish up with one of the guest bedrooms, and that will be it for today."

"Where do you want me to start?" Laura asked.

"I'd like you to arrange them by category, you know, put all of the silver ones together, then all of the cut glass, and so on. That will make it easier for me when I research them."

A few hours later Rosa knocked on the door, even though it was open. "I'm sorry to bother you, but I didn't want to startle you and have you drop one of those perfume bottles. Mrs. Jensen loved that collection."

"I'm not surprised. It's a superb collection. What can I help you with?" Marty asked.

"Mrs. Bolen is here and would like to talk to you. She says it's important."

Marty raised her eyebrows in surprise. "Really? That's kind of thought-provoking. I can't imagine what it's about. Would you tell her I'll meet her in the breakfast nook in a minute? I'm down to the last one of these perfume bottles, and I'd like to finish up, so I don't lose my train of thought."

"Marty, why don't you talk to her alone? She didn't ask for me, and it may be a private conversation. I'll stay here and put the bottles back just the way we found them. I can take some photographs of the items in the guest bedroom. It looked like it was just furniture, a couple of rugs, and some paintings. You can finish up after you talk to her. Okay?"

"That would be a big help. I really don't want to stop what I'm doing to talk to her, but if she came out here to talk to me, I probably better make the time," Marty said as she walked out of the room.

Nikki was sitting in the breakfast nook sipping a glass of the pomegranate rickey Rosa had served them at lunch. She was just as beautiful and just as impeccably dressed as she had been yesterday. A simple turquoise sleeveless linen sheath hugged the curves of her body, making the dress appear to have been custom made for her. Silver bracelets, earrings, and rings with turquoise pieces studding them accented her dress as well as her dark hair which had been woven by her hairdresser with auburn strands. She was a stunningly beautiful woman, and she knew it.

She looked Marty up and down as Marty approached the table. Marty read the silent disapproval and felt like she not only belonged back in the Midwest, but probably should have been in one of the barns back there. Nikki looked every bit the uptown girl and next to her, Marty felt like she was a "farm girl."

Well, I am what I am, Marty thought. *Might as well get this over with as fast as I can.*

"Good afternoon, Nikki. What can I do for you?"

"Sorry if I appeared to be giving you the once over, but I was. You really should consider getting your hair styled by a good hairdresser. It would be a start and would help you a lot. I'll make this brief. The only reason I'm here is because Pam was my best friend. I called Jeff this morning to talk to him. He and I have been out to dinner quite a few times, and I was under the distinct impression it was more than a casual relationship. Evidently I was wrong. He told me he didn't want to see me anymore, and that he was interested in someone else. I asked him if I knew that someone else, and he told me it was you. Sorry, Marty, but I'm having a hard time thinking you're more appealing to a man than I am, but that's what he told me."

Jeff thinks I'm more appealing than this vision, Marty thought incredulously. *Think the man needs to have his eyes checked. I would have bet the farm that the two of them were probably an ongoing item and that last night was nothing more than a hiccup in his social life. Maybe not.*

"Anyway, that's history. I have enough men interested in me that you're more than welcome to him. This is the reason I'm here. I met a friend for lunch at Mai Tai Mama's today. Pam and I met there almost weekly for years, and I know everyone who works there. The hostess, Jill Lakey, was visibly upset when I got there. I know her well enough that I asked her what was wrong. She told me that the owner, George Ellis, had really been acting strange the last few days. Jill knew he and Pam had been seeing one another, and she wondered if he was grieving over her death."

"If he'd been seeing her, I wouldn't think that was particularly unusual," Marty said.

"Nor would I. Jill told me that a few minutes before I'd gotten there she'd knocked on his office door to see if she could bring him something to drink. She'd seen him go into his office, so she knew he was in there, but he didn't answer her knock, and so she walked in. He was seated at his desk, and there were a bunch of small china figurines on it. She thought that was really strange. She asked him if she could get him anything, and he was furious she'd come into his office without his consent. He screamed at her to get out, or he'd fire her. She ran out of the room."

"I probably would have left too if someone had screamed at me to get out of their office."

"Yes, but here's the thing I need to tell you and you probably need to tell Jeff, since he won't accept my calls. I tried calling him with this information, but it went to voicemail, and I know he monitors his calls. It was obvious he didn't want to talk to me. Jill told me she'd never seen anything like those little figurines. I asked her what was so unusual about them, and she told me they were little monkeys all dressed up in old time costumes and playing musical instruments." Nikki sat back and watched Marty's reaction.

"The Monkey Band," Marty gasped. "Do you think it was the Monkey Band that's missing from here?"

"I have no idea, but I think it's really a strange coincidence that George would have been seeing Pam for several months, Pam breaks it off, and then after she's murdered he suddenly has a Monkey Band set. I'm sure Pam would have told me if he had a Monkey Band set. I know she liked him, but that was it. After Brian's death she told me she would never marry again, because Brian had been the love of her life. What do you think?"

"I don't know what to think," Marty said, "but I certainly agree that it's strange. I'll mention it to Jeff. I'm sure it might very well have some bearing on this case."

Nikki stood up and said, "I'd say it was nice seeing you again, but we both know that would be a lie. Enjoy Jeff. He's a nice man." She turned and in a loud voice said, "Goodbye Rosa, I'll let myself out."

Marty stood for a moment before she went into the guest room, knowing that what Nikki had just told her was important, but not sure where it fit into the murder of Pam Jensen and the theft of the Monkey Band.

CHAPTER TWENTY-TWO

"We're at a good stopping place," Marty said, "Let's call it a day. We can finish this tomorrow. The main thing tomorrow will be the Meissen collection and the furniture and art in the living room. There are a couple of other rooms we haven't done yet, but they're not a problem. I have a book expert coming to appraise the antique books, and he's going to meet us here at nine tomorrow morning. That should give him plenty of time. I'll be glad when this one's over. Way too much drama for me."

"I agree. While you're doing a quick scan of your photos, I'll tell Rosa we're leaving."

They walked out the door to Marty's car with Rosa following. Rosa turned around and went back in the house. "Go ahead, I need to turn on the alarm," she said. She came out of the house, waved to them, and began walking towards the bus stop.

Laura looked to Marty and said, "See that car over there. It's probably a psychic thing, but I think it's following Rosa, and she doesn't look the least bit nervous. I've got a feeling it's the police, and they're watching her. Maybe she told Jeff something that led him to believe she needed police protection."

"Come on, Laura. Police protection? That's a pretty big stretch, even for you. I know Jeff was going to talk to her, and maybe it has to do with that. If it turns out it is police protection, I'll owe you a big apology." They put the camera equipment into the trunk and got into the car. Marty turned to Laura. "You've been here with me for two days. Any thoughts on who did it?"

"Well, one thing I'm noticing is that Rosa looks like the weight of the world has been lifted off her shoulders. We'll have to ask Jeff what happened during their talk."

"I'm glad. She seems like a very nice woman. I'm sure Jeff has to talk to everyone connected with the case, but I'd hate to hear she had anything to do with it."

"She didn't."

"How do you know?" Marty asked.

"Same way I always know. I just know. Just like I know the car following her is police protection for her. Now tell me what Nikki wanted to talk to you about."

Marty related the conversation she'd had with Nikki and concluded with, "I'm glad she told me. It does indeed sound strange that George would have possession of a Monkey Band set."

Laura was quiet for a moment. "You need to tell Jeff about that. Somehow that's a very important part of the case."

"What makes you say that? I agree, it's weird this George Ellis guy would suddenly have a Monkey Band set when one was stolen out of Mrs. Jensen's house, but I sure can't see him doing anything to harm Pam Jensen. Remember, he wanted to marry her. You usually don't murder someone you want to marry, right?"

"Maybe if you'd been thinking your whole life you were going to marry a certain woman, and then she tells you she has no intention of marrying you, you might do whatever is necessary in order to make sure that no one else ever marries her if you can't have her."

"Laura, that's a little farfetched even for you. You don't seriously think that the man who wanted to marry her was also the person responsible for killing her?"

"It may be farfetched, but the spirits or whatever in the heck you want to call them, are telling me he needs to be investigated. I strongly suggest you tell Jeff, and if you don't, I will."

"Well, you don't need to get all high and mighty on me. I'll tell him. Anyway, he's coming for dinner tonight."

"I'm well aware of that. If you remember, I was the one who had to ask him, because you were afraid of what your friendly neighbors in the compound would think if you did."

"I'm beginning to think it's a good thing I've never taken you on any of my appraisals before this one. I'm beginning to think it's affecting your common sense."

"I think it is, too. Let's hope you don't have any more appraisals where the owner gets killed, and one of the victim's collections is missing and playing a major role in solving the murder."

"Laura, we don't have any proof she was killed for the Monkey Band. At this point, it's sheer conjecture."

"It's not only sheer conjecture, I'm actually certain that was not the reason for her death."

"So you think it was a random thing. Someone just happened to gain access to her house, offed her, and then stole the Monkey Band set. Please Laura, that's a little hard to swallow."

"Maybe so, Sis, but when this is over and done with, I'd like you to think back to this conversation and remember what I said about the Monkey Band not being the reason for her death."

"So you think the theft of the Monkey Band was collateral damage?" Marty asked.

"Yup, that's what I think," she said, crossing her arms.

"Well, you're entitled to believe whatever you want. Anyway, I need to stop at the Hi-Lo drug store and pick up the photos I uploaded to their photo department last night."

"Since we don't have to cook again tonight, no problem," Laura said. "I need to pick up some eye drops anyway. I love living here, but this desert air really affects my dry eye syndrome. As long as I wear my contact lenses, I'm fine, but when I wake up in the middle of the night and in the morning, I can barely get my eyes open. Feels like sandpaper."

"I had no idea it was that bad. I'm sorry, Laura. I'm going to change the subject, but I have to tell you how much I love this little town of High Desert. I mean, look at the buildings. They're old-time, not some modern monstrosity. Everybody keeps their houses and offices up beautifully. It has a great deal of charm. We've got all the basics here like a doctor, a dentist, and those types of services. And I love the market. It's a real market where people come into town and bring what they grew in their gardens, although that's not so easy to do in the desert. The owner of the market even puts colorful plants in the flower beds next to the entrance. You never see that in big cities, but I think what I like best of all is that the people here are real people. Every time I'm in Palm Springs, all I want to do is get back here and be around people like Max, people who have lived here all their lives and can't imagine living in some big city and probably wouldn't be able to survive if they did."

"I know exactly what you mean," Laura said. "I never thought I'd be happy in a town that has one main street, one church, and one market, but I feel so lucky I stumbled on this place. I find the local residents to be absolutely charming. They don't have pretenses, and even though I'm a newcomer they've accepted me. Wherever I go, they greet me and sincerely seem to care how I'm doing. After living here, I can't imagine living anywhere else."

Marty pulled into a parking space in front of the Hi-Lo drug store and said, "This may not be healthy, but I also love this drug store.

When's the last time you ever had a pharmacist ask you if you could tell him about a Victrola record player he inherited from his grandfather? It's wonderful." They opened their car doors, stepped out, and walked into the store.

CHAPTER TWENTY-THREE

"Meet you in the car. I left it unlocked," Marty said to Laura as she walked over to the photo department. "Hey, Lucy. Good to see you. I trust you got the photos I uploaded to you last night and my photographs are ready."

"Sure thing, Marty," Lucy said looking around to make sure no one could hear her. "Know I'm not s'possed to look at the photos, but ya' always got the best. Purtier things than I've ever seen. Lawdy, some of that furniture, guess it was in the dinin' room, jes' 'bout took my breath away. Ain't never seen nothin' like that. Must be somethin' bein' an appraiser."

"I'm very lucky. I really enjoy what I do, and I really appreciate the job you do for me with these photographs. I need them to be very glossy and very clear so the marks and some of the things like mortise and tenon joints show and can substantiate the age of a piece. You always manage to make me look good, and I want to thank you."

"Ain't no need to thank me. Jes' doin' my job. Gonna' send me some more tonight?"

"Yes, I'll transfer the pictures I took today from my camera to my computer and send them to you."

"Whatcha' see today?"

"Well, normally for confidentiality purposes, I never discuss my appraisal or who I did it for, but since you're going to look at the photos no matter what I say," Marty grinned, "get prepared to see some of the oldest and most beautiful perfume bottles I've ever seen."

"Ya' mean people have enough money they can collect somethin' like perfume bottles? Man, guess I better be a little more careful 'bout that Avon bottle Jake gave me for Christmas."

"Uh, Lucy, these are not store bought brand name bottles, they're containers which fine perfumes were put in with most of them dating from the 18th century."

"Well, dang it all. Had my heart goin' fer' a minute jes' thinkin' I could get rich offa that Avon perfume. Never can 'member the name. It's some fancy schmancy Frenchy name. 'Member it means water."

"In that case it would probably be '*eau*' of something. That's the French word for water."

"Ya' know, ya' ain't the only one who has me develop pictures of old things. Ol' Randy, ya' know the one who lives in that shack outside of town with the shed behind it?"

"I don't think I've ever met him," Marty said, "but yes, I know the shack you're talking about."

"No big loss. He's kinda mean, but man ya' outta see the pictures he gets developed here. Got lots of Injun stuff, ya' know some pieces of pottery, headdresses, and beaded belts. Think that meanness comes because he's lonely. Used to live with Marty BirdSong, but he kicked her out awhile ago. Comes inta town some Saturday nights and gets all drunked up over at the Road Runner Bar. I kinda like that bar, and some Saturday nights Jake and I go in and have a coupla of brewskies. That's when I seen him."

"I was in there once, and it does have a lot of local flavor. Tell me more about Randy. I'm curious."

"Well," she said, looking around again. "Ya' didn't hear it from me, but one time Jake and I were sittin' at the bar and Randy was talkin' to some dude 'bout sellin' him some of his stuff. Didn't hear much but 'member he was tellin' the dude that his stuff was real Injun stuff. Said he was always worried the feds would come and take it away from him. Don't know whatever happened 'bout that. He's a strange bird. Want me to tell him yer' some hot shot appraiser?"

"No, thanks. I'd rather you didn't. Sounds like he knows the value of what he's selling, although I remember reading something about certain Native American items being illegal to either sell or possess, particularly if they were found and removed from federal government land or burial sites."

"Oh, I jes' 'membered hearin' somthin' else that night. Ol' Randy told this dude he'd found a cave where the Injuns had kept their stuff, and he was the only one who knew 'bout it. Kinda got my interest up with that one."

"I can see where it would. Sounds like something out of a novel. If we're ever in here at the same time, I would like to meet him. He must be quite a character."

"That he is, ceptin' for his meanness I've always liked him. Gives me a tip every time he comes in. None of the other customers do that. Kinda surprisin' comin' from him. Always wondered 'bout it."

Sweetheart, I think the tips he gives you might just be called insurance, hoping you won't tell anyone what's in the photographs you're developing for him. Obviously you missed the memo on that.

"Lucy, I've got to go. We have a dinner guest coming to dinner tonight out at the compound, and John's cooking up some new dish. He doesn't like it if I'm late for dinner. See you tomorrow night. As always, thanks!"

"Can't wait to see them perfume bottles. Tell John ya' got somethin' to do before you eat, like sendin' me them photos," she said laughing.

Marty walked out of the store and saw Laura sitting in the car waiting for her.

"Got them, now home for another fantastic John meal. Any idea what tonight's is going to be?"

"I thought he said something about Cuba, but I could be mistaken."

"Sounds good, of course anything John makes is wonderful."

CHAPTER TWENTY-FOUR

"Laura," Marty said as she got out of the car and looked at her watch, "I've just got time to get the photos we took today downloaded onto my computer and send them over to Lucy at the Hi-Lo Drugstore. I'd like to pick them up tomorrow after we finish the appraisal. While I was talking to Lucy, I had a quick look at the ones we did yesterday, and so far, everything looks good."

"I'm glad to hear that. I could use a shower. Meet you in the courtyard."

Marty sat down at her computer and downloaded the photos she'd taken during the day from her digital camera and sent them to Lucy, knowing full well that Lucy would look at each one and probably compare her Avon perfume bottle with the perfume bottles in the photographs.

She paused for a moment and thought about Lucy and her Avon perfume bottle. It brought back memories of an appraisal Marty had done many years ago, actually it was her first appraisal. She'd been so nervous that she wouldn't be able to identify what something was, and then she had to laugh when she realized her first appraisal was going to be nothing but Avon products. The owner had made her home into a museum for Avon products. They filled the bookcases, shelves, kitchen counters, bathroom counters, and the woman even had special Lucite stands built to display what she considered to be the most important ones in her collection.

I remember thinking I'd spent all that time in college taking art history courses, spent money traveling all over the United States taking courses that were required in order for me to become certified, and here my very first appraisal was an Avon collection. When I told the woman what my fee was I felt a little guilty, because my fee was more than the items I'd appraised, but the woman hadn't cared. She was infatuated with her Avon pieces and the fact that now she could tell people her collection was so important she had to have it appraised was all she'd cared about. People! So many define themselves by their "stuff." I'd never realized how many until I started appraising.

She heard voices coming from the courtyard, so she quickly changed clothes, and joined the others. "Good evening," she said as she looked around at Jeff, John, Les, Max, and Laura. "Sorry I'm a couple of minutes late, but I had to get some photographs downloaded and sent to the drug store so they could be developed, and I could pick them up tomorrow. Anyway, looking at the full glasses in front of you, you obviously didn't wait for me," she said, laughing as she poured herself a glass of wine.

"How did the appraisal go today?" Jeff asked.

"We got quite a bit done, and we'll finish tomorrow. After dinner, I'd like to talk to you about a situation that came up. Since it falls into the realm of the murder investigation, I probably should only tell you."

"Aw, Marty, that's not fair," John said. "We're all really interested in it."

"No, Marty's right," Jeff said. "It's been my experience when a person is aware of a little known fact about a crime, it's very easy for them to innocently say something to someone, and it could cost us an arrest or worse. There are some things I'd like to talk to you about as well, Marty, but for now let's just enjoy what I'm sure will be another fabulous dinner. I can't believe my good fortune in getting invited here two nights in a row. John, what do you have for us tonight?"

"I was watching television a couple of nights ago and there was a movie on about a food truck in Florida that had made a name for itself because of the sandwich it specialized in. It was called a Cubano sandwich, and it's made with slices of marinated pork shoulder. I've had Cubano sandwiches before, but this one's a little different. I marinated the pork shoulder that goes on the sandwich for twenty-four hours in a citrus type of marinade. I had a couple of slices after I baked it, and I have to say it's really tender and tasty. Of course the fact I studded it with a lot of garlic slices didn't hurt."

"Okay," Laura said, "you've piqued my curiosity. What else goes on it?"

"Black Forest ham, sandwich pickles, Swiss cheese, butter, and mustard. It's a lot simpler to make than most of the things I serve. We'll see how you like it."

"John," Max said. "When ya' tol' me 'bout it yesterday when we was serving people downtown, I went home and made one. Course I didn't have no time to marinate the pork, so I just cooked a pork chop and sliced that sucker up, and man, gotta tell you, even without that slow cooked pork, it was one good belly thumper. And I just used them ham slices that are processed, not that fancy Black Forest ham."

"Glad to hear that. Actually, since Marty and Jeff need to do some business after dinner, I think I'll go in the kitchen and get started. Max, you can give me a hand." The two of them walked into John's house. They returned a half hour later with John carrying a huge platter of Cubano sandwiches, and Max following him with halves of fruit-stuffed cantaloupes on a large serving dish.

"John, this looks wonderful, and the cantaloupe halves with fruit inside looks delicious," Marty said.

"The cantaloupe is something I serve at The Red Pony. I mix raspberries, chopped apricots, and strawberries together, and mix them with some whipped cream cheese and a little brown sugar. Then I pack the mixture into the cantaloupe. It's really refreshing on a hot day, and you know how many of those we have here in the desert. Now, as the Italians would say, *mangia, mangia,* or eat, eat!"

Everyone was quiet for a few moments and then Les was the first to speak. "John, this may be the best sandwich I've ever had. I know I shouldn't, but I'm going to have another one, even if I do have to work tomorrow. The combination of flavors is great."

"Thanks. So you think I should put it on the menu?" John asked.

There was a resounding chorus of yeses as hands reached out for their second Cubano sandwich.

"I'm so glad you like it. When I was looking at the movie, I thought it would be tasty. I'll buy several pork shoulders tomorrow and start marinating them."

An hour later, John said, "Max, would you help me clear the table and do the dishes? I need to load the truck a little early tomorrow. We'll be delivering some boxed lunches to a company on our way into town, so I have to get up early and assemble them."

"No sweat, Boss. I can come over here and help ya'. Ain't no skin off my back to get up an hour early. I kinda like the quiet you find early in the mornin' in the desert."

"That would be great. You can leave your car here, and as soon as we finish making the boxed lunches, and we have to make forty of them, so it's going to take a little while, we'll head out. Should give us plenty of time. While you're making the boxed lunches, I can do some prep work for the lunch crowd at The Red Pony."

"I'm on it, Boss. Don't ever need to worry 'bout stuff like that when I'm here." He followed John into his house, loaded with plates and cutlery.

"Laura," Les said as he stood up. "I finished a painting today, and I'd like you to take a look at it."

"I'd love to," she said following him into his house.

It was quiet in the courtyard for the first time that evening. "It's so beautiful tonight, mind if we stay out here and talk?" Jeff asked Marty.

"Actually, I was going to suggest exactly that. Think there's some saying about great minds…"

"Think alike," Jeff said, grinning.

CHAPTER TWENTY-FIVE

"Do you want to go first, or do you want me to?" Marty asked, after the others had left, and they were sitting alone at the picnic table in the courtyard.

"Why don't you start?" Jeff said. "And by the way, this conversation is not to be repeated."

"Jeff, one of the things I learned early on when I started appraising was the importance of maintaining confidentiality. I lock my appraisals up in a file cabinet, put the computer files on a thumb drive, and never talk about them to anyone other than in a very, very general way. It's quite a responsibility when you know who has really good things and where they live. I'm sure there are a lot of unsavory people who would like to have the information I have, so they could commit a burglary. It's kind of a heavy burden."

"I'm sure it is, and I wonder if all appraisers are as honest as you are. I would think there's a lot of money to be made by letting that confidential information get into the wrong hands."

"That's probably true, but I've never had to deal with it. Okay, I'll get started. Nikki Bolen visited me this afternoon at the Jensen home."

His right eyebrow shot up and he lowered his head and looked into his almost empty glass. "I hope I wasn't the cause of that visit."

"Yes and no. She said you told her you wouldn't be seeing her again…"

Jeff interrupted her. "You and I haven't really gotten to know each other that well. I think I mentioned the other day that I was divorced many years ago while I was still working in La Quinta. There were a number of reasons for the divorce. We married when we were just out of college, kids really, and grew to have different interests and different ways we wanted to lead our lives. She was adamant about having a family. I was just as adamant about not having children. I've seen too many of my colleagues shot or hurt in the line of duty. I made a vow I would never have children, because there was always the chance that something might happen to me. I couldn't have children knowing there was a chance they might be raised without a dad."

"Oh, Jeff. What a tragedy that you even have to think about things like that."

"Anyway, after five years of being married we got divorced. There was no rancor, we didn't hate each other, in fact we've actually remained good friends and even talk now and then. She remarried and has three children. That's what she always wanted, and she's happy. I have no children, never remarried, and thought I was happy until I met you yesterday. Nikki and I have been seeing each other for the last couple of months. No, I'm wrong. Might as well be honest with you. I'd want you to be honest with me and starting out a relationship with dishonesty is not the way I want ours to develop.

"We weren't just seeing each other, we were having a torrid affair, an affair I ended this morning. I have no idea what happened when I met you, but there was something about your warmth and easygoing manner that made me want to know you much better. Nikki's perfect cosmetically enhanced body and face seemed so totally false after I met you. Anyway, I just wanted you to know the background."

"Well," Marty said, "while we're talking about the past, might as well tell you my story. I thought I had a perfect marriage. We'd been married for twenty-five years when my husband told me he wanted a divorce, so he could marry his secretary. My perfect world in a small town in the Midwest crashed. After he told me, I understood why conversations always stopped when I walked into a room or a store. I had to be the only one in town who didn't know about the affair. I didn't know what to do or where to go. About that time Laura called and told me she knew Scott and I were getting divorced."

"She knew about you getting divorced? How?"

"I have no idea. It's that psychic thing she has. Anyway, she told me there was going to be an opening here in the compound, and she wanted me to come out here to live. She also told me she was sure I could get some appraisal referrals from the insurance company where she works. I shipped my books and some clothes to her and drove out here a few days later. I've never regretted it, and I've grown to love this funky little town of High Desert and this compound where I live with the others."

They were both quiet for a few moments and then Marty spoke. "Jeff, I'm glad you ended your relationship with Nikki. I'd like to get to know you better."

He put his hand on hers and said, "Marty, at our age I really don't want to spend a lot of time doing some requisite 'get to know you' dance. Pure and simple, I want to see where this goes, because I think it's definitely going to go places. That doesn't mean I'll go caveman and drag you into your house and throw you on the bed, but it does mean I'm not going to wait a couple of years for permission to really kiss you. By the way, has Laura said anything about us? She probably knows more about our relationship than we do," he said with a twinkle in his eye.

"No, but might be worth asking. Okay, let's get back to business. Here's what Nikki had to say." She told Jeff about George Ellis and the Monkey Band that Jill had seen in his office earlier that afternoon. "I haven't wanted to think this, but if Pam Jensen told George she wasn't going to marry him, and it totally shocked and angered him because he'd been counting on it, do you think he could be the one who murdered her and stole the Monkey Band set?"

"I don't know, but I think based on what you just told me I might be able to get a search warrant for his office. Even though I'm the detective on the case, it's obviously a police investigation. I'll go to my sergeant and ask him to request a warrant from the judge who issues warrants for cases like this. I'll call him when we finish," Jeff said.

"I remember Laura telling me she had a feeling or a vision that while the Monkey Band would play an integral part in Pam Jensen's death, it wasn't the reason for her death. If she's right, George might have killed her because she wouldn't marry him, and in order to make the killing look like a burglary gone bad, he stole the Monkey Band to try and cover up the murder he'd committed."

"That's a strong possibility considering she was right about Rosa."

"What do you mean?"

"Remember, Laura said she sensed guilt coming off of Rosa. Well, let me tell you about the conversation that Rosa and I had." He spent the next twenty minutes telling her.

When he'd finished, Marty said, "This is so sad. No wonder people sometimes engage in some sort of criminal conduct that you wouldn't normally expect of them. Often it's not because they're bad people, but circumstances force them to take actions they normally would never do. Rosa's taking money to not turn on the security system is sure a case in point. I hope her granddaughter is going to be okay. This revelation by Rosa certainly gives another angle to the case. Maybe it wasn't George, and instead it was the guy Rosa told you about, this man named Lou. The murder did happen the night Rosa left without turning the security system on. Maybe Pam Jensen surprised him while he was trying to steal the Monkey Band, and he had to kill her. Are you going to arrest Rosa?"

"In answer to your question about Rosa, I won't know until we find out who did it. She may have left without turning the security system on, but it might not have been Lou who committed the murder. Both Lou and George seem like viable suspects. And don't forget about Pam's son, Jim, and Henry Siegelman. Her son stood to gain a lot with her death, and while I don't for a minute think Henry would ever dirty his hands by personally committing a theft or a murder, he certainly could have hired Lou or even someone else. As things stand now, we don't know who Lou was working for."

"Are all your cases this convoluted?" Marty asked.

"No, and this really is one of the more challenging ones. You've got a great deal of money at stake in the form of a large inheritance, a love affair that went bad, at least on one side, a housekeeper who took a $50,000 bribe to arrange for the security system to be off, and several people desperate to possess a very expensive and rare antique set. Yes, it's a very challenging case. I really don't want to leave, but tomorrow is going to be a busy day for me, particularly if I can get a judge to issue the search warrant I'll be requesting. Maybe I can put this case to bed tomorrow, so I can concentrate on a certain woman I met yesterday."

"You know, I think I'd like that," Marty said as they walked to the gate. She reached her arms around his neck and kissed him gently at first, and then passionately. Jeff returned the kiss with force and pressed his body against hers. After a moment, she pushed him away. "You've got a murder and a theft to solve, and I have an appraisal I have to finish, but rather than Laura asking, I'll ask. Any chance you can come to dinner tomorrow night?"

"Actually, I was already planning on it. Sleep well." He grinned and gave her a half salute as he got into his car.

Marty walked into her house, shaking her head in disbelief at the way her life had changed in the last year, especially in the last two days.

Wasn't planning on meeting a man and having feelings like this. It's crazy, but I'm liking it.

CHAPTER TWENTY-SIX

"We've got to stop meeting like this," Marty said the next morning, as she and Laura walked out the front doors of their respective homes at the same time.

"Don't know about you, but I'll be glad when this is over. It's been quite fascinating, but Dick called last night wanting to know how much longer it was going to be before the appraisal was completed. He told me my desk was overflowing with work which is exactly what I did not want to hear. At least I'm getting paid while I'm accompanying you and holding up the tape measure. Somehow, I think this is a waste of my intelligence."

"We'll finish up today. May be a waste of your intelligence, but you sure were a help when it came to that diamond ring. I'm not sure poor Carl will ever get over that experience. Please don't do it again. Sometimes your powers scare even me."

"Don't think I'll need to use any more of my powers on the appraisal. I didn't see anything that looked like it needed my help. Glad you feel we'll finish up today. Let's do it."

It was particularly hot for October. The weatherman had predicted a high temperature of 107 degrees for the day. The heat shimmered on the desert floor as Marty and Laura drove down the hill from High Desert to the Jensen residence.

The antique book appraiser was waiting for them by the gate. Marty rang the buzzer on the gate, and Rosa immediately unlocked it and opened the front door for them. Marty introduced him to Rosa. "I heard you say yesterday you would be able to wrap up the appraisal today. Do you think that's possible?" Rosa asked.

"Yes, unless something happens that's totally unforeseen. By the way Rosa, I don't know the terms of the Will, but I'm wondering what you're going to do when the house is closed up?"

"I was planning to look for work when you finished the appraisal, but I received a phone call from Mrs. Jensen's stepdaughter, Amy, this morning. She told me she was going to give some of the money from her share of the estate to her stepbrother, Jim, and his sister Marilyn, and in return they will give her their share of the house and the antiques. She asked me to stay on and work for her. She's even giving me a raise in salary. I can't tell you how happy this makes me!

"Amy thought the house should be kept in the family, so she's going to keep it and not sell it. I've met her many times, and I like her. She's very involved with a lot of charity causes. She's kind of like Mrs. Jensen in that respect. Mrs. Jensen was a large donor to a number of them. I'm so glad I can stay here, because I love working here."

"So her stepbrother, Jim, didn't want the house?"

"No. She said he was so distraught after hearing about the terms of the Will his mother had drawn up reducing his inheritance to one-fourth instead of the one-half he was expecting, that he's decided to move out of Palm Springs and go to San Francisco. It's kind of funny because Amy lives in San Francisco, and she's going to move to Palm Springs. She told me she's always wanted to write a book and that as peaceful and quiet as it is here in the desert, she might finally be able to do it."

"I'm glad for you. Well, enough talking. We need to get started if we're ever going to finish the appraisal today. Our main focus will be on the living room. Between the Meissen collection and a number of other good pieces of furniture and decorative items, we'll be there until at least mid-afternoon."

After the antique book appraiser had finished, Rosa served them lunch in the breakfast nook. It was the time in an appraisal that Marty always loved, the downhill side. They'd finished the Meissen collection and most of the other decorative items in the living room when Marty's phone rang. Jeff's name came up on the phone monitor. "Good afternoon. How is your day?" she asked.

"It's fine, but I'm in a hurry. We'll talk tonight. I was able to get a search warrant and went to George's restaurant. The hostess let me into his office. I found the Monkey Band set as well as a .9mm gun…"

Marty interrupted him. "Wasn't that the type of gun that was used to kill Pam Jensen?"

"Yes, and please don't interrupt again. Just listen to me. I took the gun to our ballistics lab and told them I had to have a test run on it ASAP to see if it there was a match with the gun involved in the murder. I got the results a few minutes ago. It's a match. Why I'm calling is this. You told me the other night that Carl, the antique dealer, had been called by someone wanting to know the value of a Monkey Band set. From what you told me, he was unable to get the man's name. You must have mentioned to Carl that I was the detective working on the case. Anyway, he called me a little while ago and said a man had brought one of the pieces from the Monkey Band set, the conductor, into his shop. The man told Carl he'd inherited the set from his recently deceased mother and wanted to know what it was worth."

"Did Carl find out who he was?"

"No, but the security camera in the store was able to photograph the man. When Carl called me, I immediately went over and looked at it. I've seen a number of photographs of George Ellis, and it was him. Here's why I'm calling. Carl told George that he would have to do some research on it, and he would get back to him in a few days.

George told him he couldn't wait that long and wanted to know if he could recommend anyone else who could quickly tell him the value of a Monkey Band set. He recommended you."

"Oh, no! Well, at least he doesn't know where to find me."

"Fraid he does, sweetheart. George said he was familiar with your name because he'd talked to Pam's son, Jim Warren, yesterday, and Jim had mentioned you were the one who was appraising his mother's estate."

"Jeff, what does this mean?"

"It means I don't want Rosa, you, or Laura to open the gate or the front door. I'm on my way over there. You might ask Laura what she thinks."

"Jeff, Laura wants to tell me something. Just a moment."

"Tell him he better hurry because George Ellis just pulled into the driveway, and tell him I'm having a vision he has a gun on him," Laura said.

"I heard that," Jeff said. "Have Rosa make sure the doors are locked and stand away from the front door and any windows. I'll be there in a few minutes with backup."

Rosa checked the remote lock on the front door and the gate and made sure they were locked. The three of them stood on the far side of the living room, Rosa with the remote control for the gate and front door in her hand, ready to open it for Jeff.

They heard the front door open and looked at each other in astonishment. A voice cried out, "Marty Morgan, I want to talk to you. Where are you?" George Ellis burst into the living room with a gun in his hand, just as Laura had predicted. "Which one of you is Marty Morgan?" he yelled.

Marty took a deep breath and stepped forward. "I'm Marty

Morgan. Who are you?"

"Rosa knows who I am, don't you Rosa? That's probably why I'll have to kill all three of you just like I killed Pam, but first I want you to tell me how much the Monkey Band is worth, the whole set. Here's one of the pieces. I put it in my pocket, so you could see what I'm talking about."

He retrieved the piece and handed it to Marty. She knew how valuable it was and couldn't believe George was carrying it around in his pocket. "Pam always said the Monkey Band set was the most expensive thing in the house, and a lot of collectors would kill for it. I've been on the Internet and found a couple of collectors who very badly want a set like the one Pam owned. Matter of fact one of them lives just a few miles from here in La Quinta. My problem is I don't know what to ask for it, so tell me what it's worth and be quick about it. After I take it to this guy in La Quinta and get the money from him, I'm leaving. Probably go to Brazil where there's no extradition treaty with the U.S. So, how much is it worth?"

"Give me a minute. I need to examine it for nicks to see what condition it's in," she said, trying to buy some time until Jeff showed up. She looked over at Laura, who gave her a small wink. Marty didn't know what it meant, but she assumed Laura knew something that was good.

"Hurry up, I don't have all day," George said, waving the gun at her in a threatening manner.

"How did you know I was here?" Marty asked, deliberately stalling.

"I talked to Jim yesterday, and he said you were the one he'd hired to do the appraisal. Talked to an antique dealer earlier today, and he mentioned your name. Seemed like it was kismet, you know, you doing the appraisal here and the antique dealer mentioning that you knew what Meissen things were worth. So, quit stalling and tell me what it's worth."

From behind George a voice shouted, "Police! Drop the gun, or I'll shoot. I'm a crack shot, and it will only take one shot to kill you."

George's shoulders sagged and a look of resignation came over his face as he dropped his gun on the floor. "Put your hands up in the air," Jeff commanded. He turned to where his two men were standing, guns drawn. "Get his gun and handcuff him." He looked at the three women. "Are you all right?"

"Yes, but I'm shaking so badly I think I better set the Monkey Band conductor down. I'm afraid I'll drop it" Marty said.

"Rosa, I told Marty to have you make sure the front door and the gate were locked. Why didn't you lock it?"

"I did. See, I have the remote control right here. I wanted to be able to open it when you came. They were both locked."

Jeff turned to George. "You knew the security code to get in, didn't you? But of course you would as close as you were to Pam Jensen."

"I told her not to use her birthday as the code," George said. "I told her everyone used their birthday or their pet's name as their code. She laughed and called me silly. It was easy for me to get in."

"So you punched in the code for the security system the night of the murder, is that right?"

"It was a piece of cake. Sure I did."

Without drawing attention to himself Jeff shifted his eye contact to Rosa, and the two of them exchanged looks. Jeff smiled ever so slightly at her. Rosa realized that her not arming the security system the night of the murder had nothing to do with the murder. George knew the code and punched it into the security system, not knowing that it was already unarmed because she hadn't turned it on. She took a deep breath and felt relief for the first time in several days. At the same time Jeff thought there was no reason to disclose to anyone what Rosa had done. In the long run it hadn't mattered.

"Jeff," Marty said, "George admitted he murdered Pam Jensen. The three of us heard him say it."

"I did not. They're lying. I never said anything like that. I just said I knew her security code and came into her house. While I was here I discovered her body. Someone had killed her. I was afraid they'd come back for the Monkey Band set, so I took it with me for safekeeping."

"George, you better remember that story, so you can tell it to the judge and jury, but between the ballistic matches on your gun, threatening to kill these three ladies, admitting you murdered Pam Jensen, and having a stolen piece of the Monkey Band set on you, I think your version of what happened just isn't going to fly when you tell your story."

Jeff turned to the two police officers. "Take him in and book him for murder, attempted murder, and grand theft." He turned to the women. "In California, grand theft is when anything over $950.00 in value is stolen, and if what I've been hearing is true, the Monkey Band will come in way over that." The two policemen escorted George out of the house while he ranted and raved that he was entitled to an attorney.

"Are you sure you're all right?" Jeff asked them a second time. They nodded. "Well, if you're certain, I'd like to record a statement from each of you about what took place today. After that you're free to go."

Marty said, "I still need to finish up a little more on the appraisal." "Shouldn't take me more than an hour. What are you going to do about the Monkey Band set in George's office?"

"I have one of the officers getting it now. He's going to take it to the station for safekeeping. It's too valuable to be left in George's office. I want you to come to the station tomorrow and appraise it. After all, it is part of the estate. I'll take the piece George had with him to the station so the set is intact. It's gone through so much, I'd hate for anything to happen to it now."

"If you hadn't shown up when you did, I don't think any of us would be talking to you, and you'd probably be taking photos of us for the crime lab," Laura said.

Marty turned to Laura, "You winked at me when George was talking. What was that all about?"

"I knew Jeff was at the front door and everything would be all right, and it was."

"We've got the same parents. Is it possible for you to transfer a little of that psychic ability to me?"

"You're not the first one to ask, but the answer is no. I don't know how it works, but I just know it does work."

"I'll vouch for that. I was a total disbeliever in the beginning, but you've converted me," Jeff said. "Do psychics drink or eat anything special?"

"Don't know about other ones, but on a hot night like tonight a vodka tonic made with Ketel One goes down real easy."

"Meet me at the door when I show up for dinner tonight!"

EPILOGUE

LOU

Lou and his island lady, Devan, were looking out at the blue Caribbean from the porch of his condominium on Seven Mile Beach on Grand Cayman Island. Lou thought it was fitting that they were sipping on mai tais which brought back memories of the Jensen fiasco.

It cost me fifty grand, but a deal's a deal. The housekeeper left the security system off just like I'd asked. It wasn't her fault someone got to the Monkey Band set before I did and killed a woman in the process. Don't know what that was all about, but as soon as I realized what had happened, I put on one of my disguises and got the heck out of Dodge. Anyway I needed a little R and R, and the mai tais work real well on the rest part of R and R and lord knows, Devan can sure help a man relax.

Think I'll lie low down here for a couple of weeks and then head back to the States. Heard there's some good jewelry in a house in Dallas that might be open to a heist. I'm told the housekeeper there has a little gambling problem and might need a little extra money. Yeah, it's a good life.

JIM MORGAN

Jim never left Pam Springs. He bought Mai Tai Mama's from George

Ellis, who could no longer run it now that he was in jail awaiting his trial, and the judge had denied him bail.

George told Jim he'd sell him the restaurant with the caveat that when he was released from jail, because he was certain he'd be acquitted, he could buy the restaurant back for the same amount of money he'd sold it to Jim.

Everyone but George knew he was going to prison for a long, long time. His attorney had recommended he accept a plea bargain a number of times, but to no avail.

Jim discovered he was a born restaurateur. He loved greeting the customers and overseeing all of the operations of the restaurant. It had taken him a long time to figure out what he could be good at, but even Brian Jensen would have heartily approved of the way he ran the restaurant.

It even looked like he might make a marriage work, at least the hostess Jill was hoping it would work out. Life was good, finally.

HENRY SIEGELMAN

Henry searched the Internet diligently and increased the amount he paid the people who were on the lookout for him for the three pieces he needed to complete his Monkey Band set.

His great regret was that he couldn't persuade Pam Jensen's stepdaughter, Amy, to part with the set. As soon as he'd heard she was the one who would be inheriting Pam's antiques, he'd gotten in touch with her and offered her an unbelievable amount of money for the Monkey Band. She'd told him in no uncertain terms that not only was she not interested in selling it, she would never sell the Monkey Band under any circumstances. She told him she felt the set was a link to her stepmother and even her father, since he had bought it for Pam. She told him that of all the antiques she'd inherited, the Monkey Band was her favorite.

Henry spends many a night thinking and scheming about how he can get the three pieces he needs to complete his set, but so far he hasn't found a way.

ROSA

Rosa loved being Amy's housekeeper. She'd always enjoyed every minute of the days she spent in Pam Jensen's home, and everything in it was special to her. She never considered what she did as being work, just an enjoyable thing for her to do. It was Rosa who suggested to Amy that she turn the pool house into a writing area, and it proved to be a very good suggestion. Amy had just published her first book and was deep into writing the second in what might prove to be a very profitable series.

She never heard from Lou again, and she used the money he'd given her to pay for her granddaughter's operation which was one hundred percent successful. The doctors assured her that her granddaughter could now lead a totally normal life.

Because of their deep religious faith, over time she and Julio had come to think of Lou as an angel delivered to them by God from heaven above. They believed Lou was an angel in disguise while he was here on earth, but that he couldn't tell her who he really was. Simply stated, he must have been a gift from God in the form of an angel. Without Lou, Rosa knew her granddaughter's life would have turned out quite differently. What other explanation could there possibly be?

Julio had found work as a gardener for a company that specialized in the residential area where Rosa worked, so from time to time they could even have lunch together. She'd never been happier.

JEFF AND MARTY

The attraction between the two of them hadn't lessened with time, and if anything, it had grown. Jeff had become a fixture at the compound, and Marty spent many an hour listening to him talk about his latest cases. She found she enjoyed it and often gave him some of her thoughts and ideas that occasionally had actually helped him solve a case. She began to wonder if maybe she had a little of what Laura had.

In addition to the insurance company referrals, Marty was getting many referrals from people satisfied with the work she'd done for them. Jeff thought she should hire a couple of people and expand her practice, but she was happy the way things were. Scott continued to pay her a large amount of alimony each month and that, in addition to the money she made from appraising, allowed her to be free from any financial concerns.

She recognized that the alimony she was receiving could become a potential problem in her relationship with Jeff. On one hand it allowed her to do pretty much whatever she wanted, but on the other hand, if she ever married Jeff, and he had hinted at it, under the terms of the divorce, the alimony would end. She knew the day was rapidly approaching when she'd have to make a decision, but until then she'd decided to let things continue as they were – having a very attractive, attentive detective in love with her.

Hey, life could be worse, she often thought!

RECIPES

CUBANO SANDWICH (SERVES FOUR)

Marinade Ingredients

Boneless pork shoulder butt roast (5-6 pounds)
4 garlic cloves, sliced into 16 pieces
2 large onions, sliced
1 cup orange juice
1 cup lime juice
1 tbsp. ground cumin
2 tbsp. dried oregano
1 tsp. salt
1 tsp. pepper

Sandwich Ingredients

4 oval French rolls (shape of a hot dog bun)
¼ cup butter, softened
4 tbsp. Dijon mustard
8 thin sandwich dill pickle slices
¾ lb. sliced Black Forest deli ham
¾ lb. Swiss cheese slices

Directions

Cut 16 one inch slits in roast. Insert garlic slices.

In a large bowl combine onion, orange juice, lime juice, and seasonings. Reserve ½ cup marinade. Put a layer of aluminum foil on the bottom of a large shallow roasting pan to help with clean up. Put the roast in the pan and cover with the remaining marinade. Refrigerate overnight.

Preheat oven to 350 degrees. Drain marinade off of roast. Pour the reserved marinade over the roast and bake for 2 ¾ hours – 3 ¼ hours, depending on size of roast. Let stand 15 minutes before thinly slicing.

Sandwiches

Cut rolls in half lengthwise. With a serrated knife blade, trim a thin slice off the top and bottom of each roll. Spread butter on the outside top and bottom of each roll. Smear mustard over the inside top and bottom halves of each roll. Layer bottom halves of roll with pickles, pork slices, ham, and cheese. Replace tops. Cook in panini cooker or in heavy pan over medium high, turning when brown.

MEXICAN EGGS BENEDICT

Corn Bread Ingredients

2 tbsp. butter
1 cup yellow cornmeal
1 cup whole wheat flour
½ tsp. salt
2 tsp. baking powder
2 eggs
3 tbsp. honey
¼ cup cooking oil

1 cup milk

Remaining Ingredients

1 tbsp. olive oil
1 clove garlic, minced
1 can black beans, drained and rinsed
3 cups cold water
¼ cup white vinegar
½ tsp. salt
8 large eggs
½ cup shredded cheddar or Monterey jack cheese
½ cup chopped tomatoes
2 tbsp. chopped cilantro

Directions for Cornbread

Preheat oven to 450 degrees. Place the butter in 8" x 10" pyrex pan. Set in oven to melt. In large bowl, whisk the dry ingredients and make a well in the center. Whisk the wet ingredients in another bowl and mix the two together. Tilt the pan with the butter to coat all sides and bottom, and then pour batter into pan. Bake until corn bread is golden on top and begins to pull away from the edges, about 25 minutes. Cool slightly and cut into 6 to 8 squares. Set aside.

Directions for Eggs

Heat olive oil and garlic over medium heat and add beans, stirring to coat. Add ¼ cup water and simmer for 5 minutes.

Combine the 3 cups of water, vinegar, and salt in a large skillet and bring to a simmer. Crack the eggs, one at a time, into a small bowl and gently slide them into the skillet. Poach the eggs, spooning some of the water over the tops of the eggs occasionally. Cook until the whites look firm and the yolks are slightly cooked through, about 4 minutes. Using a slotted spoon, remove the eggs and transfer to a plate to drain.

To assemble the eggs benedict, place 2 squares of corn bread on each plate and top with black beans, 2 poached eggs, shredded cheese, tomatoes, and cilantro. Serve and enjoy!

PAN FRIED RIB-EYE STEAK WITH CABERNET REDUCTION SAUCE (SERVES TWO)

Ingredients

16 oz.boneless rib-eye steak (thick cut)
2 tbsp. BBQ seasoning rub (Monterey Steak Seasoning recommended)
1 tbsp. cooking oil
¼ cup shallots, rough chopped
½ cup cabernet sauvignon wine
¼ cup sliced green onions
¼ cup rosemary, chopped w/stems removed
2 tbsp. butter
1 cup mushrooms (quartered)
1 tbsp. dried herbs de Provence
1 tbsp. corn starch mixed w/two tbsp. water

Directions

Trim all excess fat off steak. Generously coat and pat both sides of steak with seasoning rub. Lightly oil 12" frying pan and pre-heat on high. When pan is hot and thin film of oil is sizzling add seasoned steak and cook for approximately 3 minutes on each side for medium. Remove cooked steak from pan, cover w/foil and set aside while sauce is prepared.

Reduce heat, add shallots and mushrooms and cook for 1 minute. Add green onions and cook for 1 minute. Add wine, increase heat to high and reduce volume by half (takes about 3-4 min's). Add butter, rosemary and herbs de Provence. Cook 2 min's. Mix corn starch and water in separate bowl until well combined. Slowly pour and stir into pan as needed until proper thickness of sauce is obtained. Cut steak in half and plate. Spoon wine sauce over steak and serve. Enjoy!

LAMB MEATBALLS WITH WARM YOGURT SAUCE

Ingredients

Meatballs
1 lb. ground lamb (look for it in frozen food section)
1 egg, lightly beaten
½ cup bread crumbs
½ cup finely diced onions
1 tsp. dried oregano
1 tsp. salt
½ tsp. ground cumin
Fresh ground black pepper to taste
1 tbsp. olive oil

Yogurt Sauce
1 cup chicken broth
2 cups plain yogurt
1 egg, lightly beaten
2 cloves garlic, grated
2 tbsp. chopped fresh dill, plus more for garnish
2 tsp. butter
½ tsp. red pepper flakes
¼ tsp ground cumin
1 16 oz. package egg noodles

Directions

Combine lamb with the next seven ingredients and mix well with your hands. Shape into 24 balls, dipping hands in cold water as needed to keep mixture from sticking. In 12" frying pan heat olive oil over medium heat. Add meat balls in single layer. (You may have to do this in two batches) Fry gently, turning with two soupspoons or tongs so they brown on all sides, about 4-5 minutes. Remove meatballs to a plate and discard any excess fat in pan. Return pan to medium-high heat, add broth, and heat for 2 minutes. Add meatballs, cover, reduce heat, and simmer for 10 minutes. Using slotted spoon return meatballs to plate.

In a large bowl whisk yogurt, egg, garlic and dill together. Slowly whisk in about ½ cup of hot broth. Pour yogurt mixture into pan, cook over medium-low heat, stirring, until sauce thickens and just begins to simmer. Add salt and pepper to taste. Add meatballs to pan, turning to coat. Cover and simmer until hot.

Boil the egg noodles per instructions on packet (approximately 10 minutes) and pour in a strainer when cooked. Place equal parts of cooked noodles in 4-6 separate bowls. Spoon meatballs and sauce on top of warm noodles.

Melt butter in small sauce pan and add red pepper flakes and cumin. Swirl until butter is foamy and aromatic. Drizzle over each portion and garnish with chopped dill. Serves 4 to 6. Enjoy!

ABOUT THE AUTHOR

Dianne lives in Huntington Beach, California with her husband Tom, a former California State Senator, and her boxer puppy, Kelly, named after the first book in the Cedar Bay Cozy Mystery Series, *Kelly's Koffee Shop*. Her passions are cooking and dogs, so when she's not cooking, she's probably playing with Kelly, who has gone from being an inquisitive puppy to a young dog that has learned what "leave it" and "no" mean, much to the relief of Dianne and Tom!

Her other award winning books include:

Cedar Bay Cozy Mystery Series
Kelly's Koffee Shop, Murder at Jade Cove, White Cloud Retreat, Marriage and Murder, Murder in the Pearl District, Murder in Calico Gold, Murder at the Cooking School

Liz Lucas Cozy Mystery Series
Murder in Cottage #6, Murder & Brandy Boy, The Death Card

High Desert Cozy Mystery Series
Murder & The Monkey Band

Coyote Series
Blue Coyote Motel, Coyote in Provence, Cornered Coyote

Website: www.dianneharman.com
Blog: www.dianneharman.com/blog
Email: dianne@dianneharman.com

Newsletter
If you would like to be notified of her latest releases please go to www.dianneharman.com and sign up for her newsletter.

Made in the USA
Monee, IL
16 June 2023

36019947R00083